This book belongs to:

Judith &
Louise Mair

The Kingfisher

CHILDREN'S COLLECTION

OF STORIES AND RHYMES

KINGFISHER

An imprint of Larousse plc
Elsley House, 24-30 Great Titchfield Street
London W1P 7AD

First published in this edition by Kingfisher 1991
4 6 8 10 9 7 5 3

A CIP catalogue for this book
is available from the British Library

ISBN 0 86272 838 X

Phototypeset by Southern Positives and Negatives (SPAN), Lingfield Surrey
Colour separations by Scantrans Pte Ltd, Singapore
Printed in China

The Kingfisher
CHILDREN'S COLLECTION
OF STORIES AND RHYMES

ILLUSTRATED BY HILDA OFFEN
STORIES RETOLD BY LINDA YEATMAN

Kingfisher

Contents

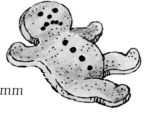

Goldilocks and the Three Bears

Once upon a time there were three bears who lived in a house in the forest. There was a great big father bear, a middle-sized mother bear and a tiny little baby bear.

One morning, their breakfast porridge was too hot to eat, so they went for a walk in the forest. While they were out, a little girl called Goldilocks came through the trees and found their house. She knocked on the door and, as there was no answer, she pushed it open and went in.

In front of her was a table with three chairs, one great big chair, one middle-sized chair and one tiny little chair. On the table were three bowls of porridge, one great big bowl, one middle-sized bowl and one tiny little bowl – and three spoons.

Goldilocks was hungry, so she sat in the great big chair, picked up the biggest spoon and tried some of the porridge from the great big bowl. But the chair was far too big and hard, the spoon was too heavy and the porridge too hot.

So Goldilocks went over to the middle-sized chair. But this chair was far too soft, and when she tried the porridge from the middle-sized bowl it was too cold. So she went over to the tiny little chair and picked up the smallest spoon and tried some of the porridge from the tiny little bowl.

This time it was neither too hot nor too cold. It was just right – and so delicious that Goldilocks ate it all up. But she was too heavy for the tiny little chair and it broke in pieces.

Then Goldilocks went upstairs, where she found three beds. There was a great big bed, a middle-sized bed and a tiny little bed. First she lay down on the great big bed, but it was very big and far too hard. Next she lay down on the middle-sized bed, but that was far too soft. Then she lay down on the tiny little bed. It was neither too hard nor too soft. In fact, it felt just right, and Goldilocks fell fast asleep.

In a little while, the three bears came back from their walk in the forest.

Father Bear looked around, then roared in a great big growly voice,

"SOMEBODY HAS BEEN SITTING IN MY CHAIR!"
Mother Bear said in a quiet gentle voice,

"Somebody has been sitting in my chair!"
And Little Bear said in a small squeaky baby voice,

"*Somebody has been sitting in my chair, and has broken it!*"

Then Father Bear looked at his bowl of porridge and said in his great big growly voice,

"SOMEBODY HAS BEEN EATING MY PORRIDGE!"
Mother Bear looked at her bowl and said in her quiet gentle voice,
"Somebody has been eating my porridge!"
And Little Bear looked at his bowl and said in his small squeaky baby voice,
"Somebody has been eating my porridge, and has eaten it all up!"
Then the three bears went upstairs. Father Bear saw at once that his bed was untidy, and he said in his great big growly voice,
"SOMEBODY HAS BEEN SLEEPING IN MY BED!"
Mother Bear saw that her bed, too, had the bedclothes turned back, and she said in her quiet gentle voice,
"Somebody has been sleeping in my bed!"
And Little Bear looked at his bed, and he said in his small squeaky baby voice,
"Somebody is sleeping in my bed, NOW!"
He squeaked so loudly that Goldilocks woke up with a start. She jumped out of bed and ran down the stairs and out into the forest. And the three bears never saw her again.

MARY'S LAMB

Mary had a little lamb,
    Its fleece was white as snow;
And everywhere that Mary went
    The lamb was sure to go.

It followed her to school one day,
    That was against the rule;
It made the children laugh and play
    To see a lamb at school.

And so the teacher turned it out,
    But still it lingered near,
And waited patiently about
    Till Mary did appear.

Why does the lamb love Mary so?
    The eager children cry;
Why, Mary loves the lamb, you know,
    The teacher did reply.

HUMPTY DUMPTY

Humpty Dumpty sat on a wall,
Humpty Dumpty had a great fall;
  All the King's horses,
  And all the King's men,
Couldn't put Humpty together again.

The Great Big Turnip

Once upon a time, in Russia, an old man planted some turnip seeds. Each year he grew good turnips, but this year he was especially proud of one very big turnip. He left it in the ground longer than the others and watched with amazement and delight as it grew bigger and bigger. It grew so big that no one could remember ever having seen such a huge turnip before.

At last the old man decided that the time had come to pull it up. He took hold of the leaves of the great big turnip and pulled and pulled, but the turnip did not move.

So the old man called his wife to come and help. The old woman took hold of the old man, and the old man took hold of the turnip. Together they pulled and pulled, but still the turnip did not move.

So the old woman called her granddaughter to come and help. The granddaughter took hold of the old woman, the old woman

took hold of the old man, and the old man took hold of the turnip. They pulled and pulled, but still the turnip did not move.

The granddaughter called to the dog to come and help. The dog took hold of the granddaughter, the granddaughter took hold of the old woman, the old woman took hold of the old man, and the old man took hold of the turnip. They pulled and pulled, but still the turnip did not move.

The dog called to the cat to come and help pull up the turnip. The cat took hold of the dog, the dog took hold of the granddaughter, the granddaughter took hold of the old woman, the old woman took hold of the old man, and the old man took hold of the turnip. They all pulled and pulled as hard as they could, but still the turnip did not move.

Then the cat called to a mouse to come and help pull up the great big turnip. The mouse took hold of the cat, the cat took hold of the dog, the dog took hold of the granddaughter, the granddaughter took hold of the old woman, the old woman took hold of the old man, and he took hold of the turnip. Together they pulled and pulled and pulled as hard as they could.

Suddenly, the great big turnip came out of the ground, and everyone fell over.

The old woman chopped up the great big turnip and made a great big pot of delicious turnip soup. There was enough soup for everybody – the mouse, the cat, the dog, the granddaughter, the old woman and the old man. There was even some left over.

A WEEK OF BIRTHDAYS

Monday's child is fair of face,
Tuesday's child is full of grace,
Wednesday's child is full of woe,
Thursday's child has far to go,
Friday's child is loving and giving,
Saturday's child works hard for its living,
And the child that's born on the Sabbath day
Is bonny and blithe, and good and gay.

GIRLS AND BOYS COME OUT TO PLAY

Girls and boys, come out to play,
The moon doth shine as bright as day.
Leave your supper and leave your sleep
And come with your playfellows into the street.
Come with a whoop and come with a call,
Come with a goodwill or not at all.
Up the ladder and down the wall,
A half-penny loaf will serve us all;
You find milk, and I'll find flour,
And we'll have a pudding in half an hour.

Cinderella

There was once a gentleman who lived in a fine house, with his kind and gentle wife and their pretty daughter. His wife died, so the gentleman married again. His new wife was not at all kind or pretty. She had been married before and had two daughters who were known, behind their backs, as the Ugly Sisters.

Although they had no reason to be unkind, the two sisters were horrid to their new stepsister. They ordered her about, scolded her and made her do all the work in the big house. Her clothes became ragged and thin and far too small. The poor girl was always cold and tired. In the evenings she would rest on a stool close to the fire, almost in the cinders and ashes.

"Cinderella. That's the perfect name for you," jeered the stepsisters when they saw her trying to keep warm.

Now the king and queen of their country had a son, and they planned a big ball for the prince in the hope that he might find a bride. Invitations were sent to all the big houses. When a large invitation card to the royal ball arrived at Cinderella's house, there was a great flurry of excitement. New dresses were chosen for the Ugly Sisters and their mother, and nobody talked about anything except the ball.

"I am sure the prince will fall in love with me," said one sister, smiling at herself in the mirror.

"You silly fool," said the other, pushing her aside. "He won't be able to resist falling in love with me. Just think, one day I could

be queen," and she pretended she was the queen already as she
ordered Cinderella to get another pair of shoes for her to try on. No
one thought of asking Cinderella if she would like to go to the ball.
They scarcely even noticed her as they rushed around trying on
different wigs, fans and gloves to go with their new ball dresses.

At last the day of the ball came, and Cinderella worked
harder than ever, helping the Ugly Sisters and her stepmother to
get ready. They quarrelled with each other all day, and by the time
the carriage drove away to the king's palace, with all the family in
it, Cinderella was glad to have some peace. But as she sat on her
stool by the fire she could not help a tear falling onto the ashes, for
she wished that she could have gone with them.

Suddenly she realized that she was not alone. A beautiful
lady stood before her with a silver wand in her hand.

"Cinderella," she said, "I am your fairy godmother. Tell me,
what are those tears for?"

Cinderella looked away.

"I wish, oh how I wish, I could have gone to the ball too."

"So you shall," said her fairy godmother, "but first we have some work to do. For if you are to go to the ball, I cannot send you as you are. Fetch me the largest pumpkin you can find in the garden."

Cinderella fetched the largest pumpkin she could see and with just a wave of her wand, her fairy godmother turned it into a gleaming golden coach.

"Now we need a few horses," said her godmother. "Look in the mouse trap and see if there is anything we can use."

Cinderella ran to the larder and found six mice running around in a cage. She watched her godmother wave her wand and suddenly, harnessed to the coach, there were six shining dappled horses, stamping their feet.

"Those horses need a coachman," decided her godmother. "Look in the rat trap, Cinderella." There were three rats in the trap and as the godmother touched the largest rat with her wand, it disappeared. But now up at the front of the coach sat a fine plump whiskery coachman in a smart uniform.

"Go and look behind the water barrel, Cinderella," said her godmother, "and see if you can find something we can use for footmen."

Cinderella ran to the water barrel and brought two lizards to her godmother. At the wave of her wand they were transformed into splendid footmen.

"There now, Cinderella, your coach is ready," said her godmother with a smile. "You will be able to go to the ball after all."

"How can I go like this?" sighed Cinderella, looking down in despair at her ragged clothes and bare feet. Her godmother touched her with her wand — her rags turned into a shimmering gown and on her feet she was wearing the prettiest pair of glass shoes she had ever seen.

As Cinderella stepped into the coach her godmother gave her a strict warning. "The magic will only last until midnight, and then everything will return to what it was before. Be sure you leave the ball before midnight, Cinderella."

When Cinderella's coach arrived at the palace the word went round that a beautiful lady had arrived in such a splendid coach that she must be a princess. The prince himself came down the steps to greet her and led her to the ballroom. As they entered, the other guests fell silent in wonder and the musicians stopped playing. The prince signalled to the musicians to play again and danced with Cinderella.

The prince stayed at Cinderella's side all evening. No one knew who she was. Not even the Ugly Sisters recognized her. Cinderella was so happy that she did not notice how quickly the time was flying by.

Suddenly she heard the clock strike the first stroke of midnight. With a cry she left the prince and ran out of the ballroom. As she flew down the steps, one of her shoes fell off, but she could not stop to pick it up.

Although the prince tried to follow Cinderella through the crowd, he soon lost sight of her. He questioned everyone carefully

but no one had seen the beautiful lady leave. The guards said that the only person who had gone out was a young raggedly-dressed girl. No one noticed the pumpkin in the corner of the courtyard or some mice, a rat and a pair of lizards that slunk into the shadows. But the prince did find the glass shoe on the steps, and he recognized it as one of the elegant shoes the mysterious and lovely lady had worn.

The next day the Ugly Sisters could talk of nothing but the beautiful lady who had captured the prince's heart and how she had disappeared so suddenly and how no one knew her name.

The palace issued a proclamation that the prince was looking for the lady who had worn the glass shoe. His servants would tour the country with it until they found the lady whose foot it fitted and the prince would marry that lady. The prince travelled around with his servants but time and again he was disappointed as the shoe failed to fit any lady's foot.

At last they came to Cinderella's house. The Ugly Sisters were waiting.

"Let me try first," cried one, holding out her foot, and pushing as hard as she could to squeeze it into the shoe. But it was no good. She gave up and laughed at her sister's efforts as she, too, tried to force her foot into the tiny glass shoe. When she had failed, Cinderella stepped forward.

"You!" sneered the Ugly Sisters. "But you were not even at the ball."

Cinderella slipped her foot into the glass shoe – it fitted perfectly. Then she drew from behind her back a second shoe which she put on her other foot. At the same moment the fairy godmother appeared and touched Cinderella with her wand. Instantly her ragged clothes changed back into the beautiful shimmering dress, and Cinderella once again became the lovely stranger.

The delighted prince asked Cinderella to marry him and Cinderella replied that there was nothing she would like more. The Ugly Sisters begged Cinderella to forgive them for their unkindness and she happily agreed. There was a fine royal wedding for Cinderella and the prince, and they lived happily ever after.

Cinderella found two husbands for the Ugly Sisters at court, and they too lived happily ever after – well, almost.

ALPHABET PIE

A was an
Apple pie

B
Bit it

C
Cut it

D
Dealt it

E
Eat it

F
Fought for it

G
Got it

H
Had it

I
Inspected it

J
Jumped for it

K
Kept it

L
Longed for it

M
Mourned for it

N
Nodded at it

O
Opened it

P
Peeped in it

Q
Quartered it

R
Ran for it

S
Stole it

T
Took it

U
Upset it

V
Viewed it

W
Wanted it

XYZ & ampersand
All wished for
a piece in hand

The Ugly Duckling

One summer's day, when the corn was golden yellow and the hay was being dried in the fields, a mother duck was sitting on her nest of eggs. She sat in the rushes of a deep moat that surrounded a lovely country manor and waited for her eggs to hatch. They were taking a very long time and she was getting very tired.

At last she felt a movement beneath her. The eggs began to crack and out popped tiny fluffy ducklings. All the eggs hatched except for one, which was larger than the rest. The mother duck was impatient to take her new ducklings swimming but could not leave the last egg unhatched. She sat, and she sat, and she sat, and just as she was about to give up, she heard a tap. Out of the egg tumbled the oddest ugliest duckling imaginable.

She took the babies into the water and proudly watched as they all swam straightaway, even the ugly duckling. She led them in a procession around the moat, showing them off to the other ducks. As they bobbed along behind her she heard many quacks of admiration and praise for her fine family. But she also heard quacks of laughter and scorn poured on the ugly duckling at the end of the line.

"He was too long in the egg," she explained. "He has not come out quite the right shape. But he will soon grow into a fine duck, just like the others."

As the weeks went by, and the corn was harvested in the fields, the ducklings grew up into ducks. But the ugly duckling with his grey feathers and clumsy shape remained different. All the ducks on the moat made fun of him and refused to let him join in their games on the water.

The ugly duckling could bear it no more. As the autumn leaves began to fall he flew away to a great marsh. There he stayed alone, hiding from the ducks among the reeds.

One day he heard a strange cry and the sound of wings in the air. Looking up he saw three dazzling white birds flying majestically overhead. The ugly duckling felt a strange longing. He did not know the name of those birds but he felt he loved them more than he had loved anything before. He watched as they passed over his head and flew beyond until they were out of sight.

Autumn turned to winter, and the ugly duckling suffered many hardships. The marshy water froze and for a while he was trapped fast in the ice. A kind man broke the ice and took him to his home, but the ugly duckling was frightened by the noise and confusion inside the house. He flapped his wings, upset a bucket of milk and fled as people shouted at him.

At last spring came, and with it warm sunshine. The ugly duckling flapped his wings. To his surprise they felt bigger and stronger, and he found he was flying easily away from the marsh towards a large and beautiful lake.

On the lake were the three wonderful birds the ugly duckling had seen flying overhead several months before. As the swans glided smoothly over the lake, he felt drawn to them, but he was sure they would tease him like the ducks because he was so ugly. He hung his head in shame.

All at once he saw a reflection in the smooth lake waters. A beautiful swan with glossy white feathers and a fine yellow beak stared up at him. He moved; the swan moved. He opened his wings; so did the swan. The ugly duckling suddenly realized – he was a swan.

The other swans swam gracefully towards him, welcoming him. Some children ran down to the lake, calling,

"Look, a new swan has appeared," and they threw bread into the water for him.

The young and beautiful swan felt quite shy with all this attention, and hid his head under his wing. But, as the lilac trees bent their branches down over the water and the sun shone warm and bright, he felt a deep happiness. He rustled his feathers, arched his sleek long neck and said to himself, "I never dreamed of such great happiness when I was the Ugly Duckling."

ON SATURDAY NIGHT

On Saturday night I lost my wife,
And where do you think I found her?
Up in the moon, singing a tune,
And all the stars around her.

PUSSYCAT MEW

Pussycat mew jumped over a coal,
And in her best petticoat burned a great hole;
Pussycat mew shall have no more milk,
Until her best petticoat's mended with silk.

IT'S RAINING

It's raining, it's pouring,
The old man's snoring;
He got into bed
And bumped his head
And couldn't get up in
    the morning.

JINGLE BELLS

Jingle, bells! Jingle, bells!
    Jingle all the way;
Oh, what fun it is to ride
    In a one-horse open sleigh.

QUEEN CAROLINE

Queen, Queen Caroline,
Washed her hair in turpentine,
Turpentine to make it shine,
Queen, Queen Caroline.

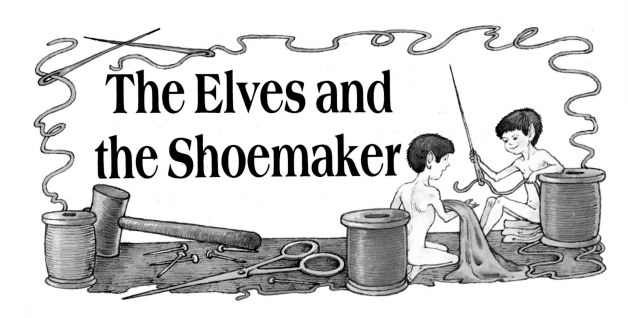

The Elves and the Shoemaker

Once upon a time there was a shoemaker who made very good shoes. But though he worked hard in his shop, times were difficult and he became poorer and poorer. One evening he realized he had only enough leather to make one more pair of shoes. He cut up the leather and laid the pieces out on his workbench to sew in the morning when the light was better.

"I may never make another pair of shoes," he sighed as he put up the shutters over his shop window.

The next morning when he went back to his workbench he found a beautiful pair of shoes. He examined them carefully and discovered they were made from the leather he had cut out the night before. The stitches were exquisite, very tiny and neat, and he knew the shoes were far better than any he could have made. Quickly he took down his shutters and placed the shoes in his shop window.

Soon the door opened and in came a grand gentleman. He bought the shoes and paid four times more than the price of an ordinary pair. With this money the shoemaker bought more leather and enough food for several days.

That evening he sat at his workbench and cut out two pairs of shoes from his new leather. He left the pieces laid out as before, all ready to sew in the morning, and put up the shutters.

In the morning he could scarcely believe his eyes, for there on his workbench were two beautiful pairs of shoes.

"Who could sew such tiny stitches?" he wondered, "and who could work so fast?"

He placed the shoes in the shop window. Rich people who had never visited his shop before came in to buy them and paid a lot of money for them.

Each night for many weeks the same thing happened. Two pairs, sometimes four pairs, were made in a night.

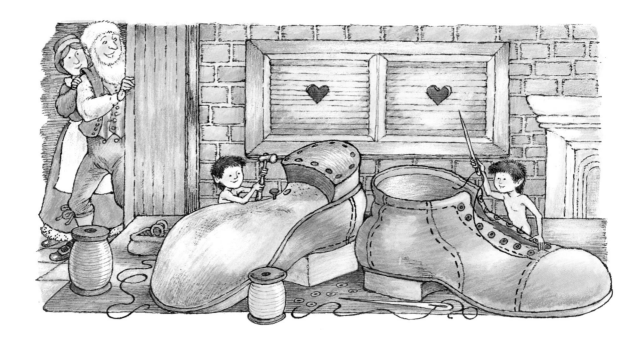

The shoemaker cut out all sorts of shoes: men's shoes, ladies' shoes, little children's shoes, dancing shoes, party shoes, shoes with laces, shoes with straps and buckles. He became well known for the excellent shoes he sold, and each week he took even more money in his shop.

One evening, just before Christmas, his wife suggested they should peep around the door of the workroom to see if they could find out who was making the shoes. As the town clock struck midnight, there was a scuffling and a scurrying by the window, and two tiny little men squeezed through a crack in the shutters and hurried over to the workbench. They took tiny tools from their workbags and began to work. They stitched and hammered, stitched and hammered, until a row of new shoes lay on the workbench. Then, their work finished, the elves left everything neat and tidy and vanished.

As it was just before Christmas, the shoemaker's wife suggested that they should give presents to the two little men who had helped them so much during the year. The next day she made two little green jackets and trousers and green hats to match, and her husband stitched two tiny pairs of boots.

The shoemaker and his wife laid these gifts out on the

workbench that evening, together with two little glasses of wine and plates with little cakes and biscuits. They then kept watch again. At the stroke of midnight, they saw the elves scramble into the workshop and climb onto the workbench as they had done before. When they saw the little green jackets, trousers and hats and tiny boots the elves gave a shout of joy. They tried on their new clothes straightaway and they were so delighted they danced around the workbench, waving their hats in the air. Then they sat down and ate all the food that had been left out, and disappeared as before.

After Christmas the shoemaker still cut out the shoes and left the pieces on his workbench but the elves never returned. They knew the shoemaker and his wife must have seen them, for their clothes were exactly the right size, and fairy people do not like to be seen. But the shoemaker was now so well known that he had plenty of customers. Although his stitches were not as tiny and neat as the elves' stitches no one ever noticed. For many years he was known as the best shoemaker in town and he and his wife were never poor again.

OLD MOTHER HUBBARD

Old Mother Hubbard
Went to her cupboard,
To fetch her poor dog a bone;
But when she got there
The cupboard was bare
And so the poor dog had none.

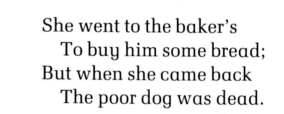

She went to the baker's
To buy him some bread;
But when she came back
The poor dog was dead.

She went to the joiner's
To buy him a coffin;
But when she came back
The poor dog was laughing.

She took a clean dish
   To get him some tripe;
But when she came back
   He was smoking a pipe.

She went to the fishmonger's
   To buy him some fish;
But when she came back
   He was licking the dish.

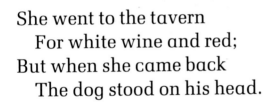

She went to the tavern
   For white wine and red;
But when she came back
   The dog stood on his head.

She went to the fruiterer's
   To buy him some fruit;
But when she came back
   He was playing the flute.

She went to the tailor's
To buy him a coat;
But when she came back
He was riding a goat.

She went to the hatter's
To buy him a hat;
But when she came back
He was feeding the cat.

She went to the barber's
To buy him a wig;
But when she came back
He was dancing a jig.

She went to the cobbler's
To buy him some shoes;
But when she came back
He was reading the news.

She went to the seamstress
  To buy him some linen;
But when she came back
  The dog was a-spinning.

She went to the hosier's
  To buy him some hose;
But when she came back
  He was dressed in his clothes.

The dame made a curtsey,
  The dog made a bow;
The dame said, "Your servant,"
  The dog said, "Bow-wow."

Nail Soup

Ο ne dark and stormy night, a tramp knocked on the door of a cottage and asked for shelter. An old woman answered the door and told the tramp sourly that he could come in if he wanted, but he must not expect any food for she had none in the house.

"And don't think you'll get a bed to sleep on either," she added, "as I only have one and that is where I sleep."

The tramp was hungry, but he could see he wasn't going to get any food, so he sat by the fire and took an old nail out of his pocket and tossed it from hand to hand.

"Do you see this nail here?" he said at last. "You'd never believe it, but last night I made the finest soup I have ever eaten by cooking this nail, and what is more I still have it to make more tonight. Would you like me to make you some nail soup?"

"Nail soup!" snorted the old woman. "I have never heard of such a thing. Don't talk nonsense." But the tramp could see she was curious.

"All I did," he told her, "was to boil it up in an old saucepan, and it was delicious."

"Well, since we have nothing else to do, and I have no food in the house, perhaps you would be good enough to show me how you do it," she said after a few moments.

"You haven't a large pot and some water, have you?" asked the tramp.

"Why yes," said the old woman, handing a big cooking pot to the tramp and showing him where the water was. She watched as the tramp carefully filled the pot half full with water, placed it on the stove, and dropped in the nail. Then he sat down to wait.

From time to time, the old woman peeped into the pot to see how the soup was doing, and once when she lifted the lid the tramp said,

"Last night all that was needed was a little salt and pepper. I don't suppose you have any in the house?"

"I might have," said the old woman ungraciously, and from a cupboard she took salt and pepper which she dropped into the water with the nail.

The next time she lifted the lid, the tramp sighed, "What a pity you haven't got half an onion for that would make the soup even better than it was last night."

"I think I might have an onion," said the old woman, quite excited by now at the thought of the nail soup, and she went to the larder to fetch an onion. As she opened the door, the tramp caught a glimpse of shelves stacked with food, but he said nothing until the onion had been in the pot for about ten minutes.

Then, stirring the soup again, he murmured to himself, "How sad that this fine onion has no carrots and potatoes to go with it." Just as he had hoped, the old woman quickly fetched some carrots and potatoes from the larder.

By now, the soup was beginning to smell good, and it was not long before the tramp said that on nights when he could add a little meat to his nail soup, it was fit even for kings and queens. In a flash, the old woman had fetched some meat for the pot.

While the soup was bubbling, the tramp looked round at the table. "It's a funny thing," he remarked, "but my nail soup always tastes better when I eat it at a table that is laid with pretty china and when there is a candle or two on the table."

The old woman, not to be outdone, put out her best tablecloth and got the best china off the dresser.

"What a shame," said the tramp, "that we have no bread to eat with this nail soup, but I remember you telling me there is no food in the house."

"I'll just look in the bread crock," said the old woman, and she pulled out a loaf that had been baked that morning.

The soup now smelled quite delicious, and the tramp was longing to eat it, but he waited a few more minutes before saying,

"I am sorry there is no wine to drink with our nail soup, as I would have liked you to enjoy it with a glass of wine."

"Just a minute," said the old woman, and she fetched a fine-looking bottle of wine from the back of a cupboard and put it on the table with two glasses.

"Now the soup is ready. I hope you enjoy it," said the tramp heartily, and he fished the nail out with a spoon and put it in his pocket before carrying the soup over to the table.

They both had a wonderful meal. After the soup, which the old woman agreed was the best she'd ever tasted, she found some cheese and other good things in the larder. They told each other many stories, laughed a lot and had a very pleasant evening.

As the candles burnt low, the old woman told the tramp to go and sleep in her bed, saying that she would be quite comfortable in a chair by the fire. They both slept soundly.

The next morning, the tramp thanked the old woman for her kindness, but she said,

"No, no, I must thank you for showing me how to make soup from an old nail."

"It's what you add that makes the difference!" said the tramp, smiling.

THE SKY

Red sky at night,
Shepherd's delight;
Red sky in the morning,
Shepherd's warning.

CONTRARY MARY

Mary, Mary, quite contrary,
　　How does your garden grow?
With silver bells and cockle shells,
　　And pretty maids all in a row.

LAVENDER'S BLUE

Lavender's blue, dilly, dilly,
  Lavender's green,
When I am king, dilly, dilly,
  You shall be queen.

Call up your men, dilly, dilly,
  Set them to work,
Some to the plow, dilly, dilly,
  Some to the cart.

Some to make hay, dilly, dilly,
  Some to thresh corn,
Whilst you and I, dilly, dilly,
  Keep ourselves warm.

The Gingerbread Man

An old woman was baking one day, and she made some gingerbread. She had some dough left over, so she made the shape of a little man. She made eyes for him, a nose and a smiling mouth all of currants, and put currants down his front to look like buttons. Then she laid him on a baking tray and put him in the oven.

After a little while, she heard something rattling at the oven door. She opened it and to her surprise out jumped the little gingerbread man. She tried to catch him, but he slipped past her, calling as he ran,

"Run, run, as fast as you can,
You can't catch me, I'm the gingerbread man!"

She chased after him into the garden where her husband was digging. He put down his spade and tried to catch him too, but the gingerbread man ran past him, calling,

"Run, run, as fast as you can,
You can't catch me, I'm the gingerbread man!"

He ran down the road with the old woman and the old man following. Soon he passed a cow. The cow called out, "Stop, gingerbread man! You look good enough to eat!" But the gingerbread man laughed and shouted over his shoulder,

"I've run from an old woman
And an old man.
Run, run as fast as you can,
You can't catch me, I'm the gingerbread man!"

He ran on with the old woman and the old man and the cow following, and soon they all passed a horse. "Stop!" called the horse. "I'd like to eat you." But the gingerbread man called out,

"I've run from an old woman
And an old man.
And a cow!
Run, run as fast as you can,
You can't catch me,
I'm the gingerbread man!"

He ran on, with the old woman and the old man and the cow and the horse following, and soon they passed some people making hay. "Stop!" they shouted. "You look good enough to eat." But the gingerbread man called out,

"I've run from an old woman
And from an old man.
And a cow and a horse!
Run, run, as fast as you can,
You can't catch me,
I'm the gingerbread man!"

He ran across the fields with the old woman and the old man, the cow and the horse and the haymakers all following. Soon he met a fox and called out,

"Run, run, as fast as you can,
You can't catch me,
I'm the gingerbread man!"

The sly fox thought to himself, "That gingerbread man looks good enough to eat," but he said nothing. He waited until the gingerbread man reached a wide deep swift-flowing river, with the old woman and the old man, the cow and the horse and the haymakers all chasing after him. Now the sly fox said,

"Jump on my back, Gingerbread Man, and I'll take you across the river!"

The gingerbread man jumped on the fox's back and the fox began to swim. As they reached the middle of the river, where the water was deep, the fox said,

"Stand on my head, Gingerbread Man, or you will get wet."

So the gingerbread man stood on the fox's head. As the current flowed more swiftly, the fox said,

"Move onto my nose, Gingerbread Man, so that I can carry you more safely. I would not like you to drown."

The gingerbread man slid onto the fox's nose. But when they reached the bank on the far side of the river, the fox suddenly went SNAP! The gingerbread man disappeared into the fox's mouth and was never seen or heard of again.

ROSES ARE RED

Roses are red,
Violets are blue,
Sugar is sweet
And so are you.

RING-A-RING O' ROSES

Ring-a-ring o' roses,
A pocket full of posies,
A-tishoo! A-tishoo!
We all fall down.

CORPORAL BULL

Here's Corporal Bull
A strong hearty fellow,
Who not used to fighting
Set up a loud bellow.

BAA, BAA,
BLACK SHEEP

Baa, baa, black sheep,
   Have you any wool?
Yes, sir, yes, sir,
   Three bags full;
One for the master,
   And one for the dame,
And one for the little boy
   Who lives down the lane.

The Story of Persephone

This story is one of the tales that the ancient Greeks told about their gods. It is the story of Persephone, the lovely daughter of Demeter, Goddess of the Harvest.

Demeter travelled around the world with Persephone, visiting all the trees and plants that produce food. As she passed by, they grew and flourished, and their fruit ripened. On hot days as she walked through a field of corn, the husks would swell and the corn would turn golden. Whenever she visited orchards and vineyards, the apples, peaches, pears and grapes would be sweet and ready to eat. Persephone would dance with joy to see how lovely the flowers looked when Demeter touched them.

One day Persephone asked her mother if she could go and play with her friends on the mountainside. Demeter agreed, but warned her not to stray too far. While Demeter visited some valleys where the harvest was late, Persephone and her friends scrambled happily over the mountainside. They found many flowers growing in the mountain meadows, and began to pick them to make garlands and chains. Further and further they wandered, until they were a long way from the valley where they had started.

Soon the meadows were shimmering in the hot mid-day sun. Persephone grew tired and dropped behind her friends. She sat down on the grass to rest while she finished the garland she was making.

Suddenly there was a great crack and a roar. The side of the mountain seemed to split open and out galloped six great black horses, pulling a gleaming black chariot. Persephone was terrified and called out, "Mother, Mother, help me!" But even as she called, the man driving the chariot leant out and swept Persephone up into the chariot. He pulled at the reins to turn the horses and they galloped back into the mountain. With another roar and a crash the gap closed, leaving no trace of what had happened.

Persephone's friends soon missed her and came back to look for her. They hunted everywhere and called and called, but there was no sign of her anywhere. At last they gave up and went back to tell Demeter.

Together they searched for hours up and down the mountain, but could find no trace of Persephone until, in the evening, they came upon a fading garland of flowers lying in the grass. Now Demeter knew that something dreadful must have happened to her daughter.

Something terrible had happened indeed. Persephone had been snatched by Hades, God of the Underworld. In his great black chariot, he drove her back to his palace of dark caverns deep inside the earth. The palace was full of beautiful things but Persephone was very unhappy there. She missed the sunlight and the flowers, and all the colours of the world she had known, and most of all she longed to see her mother. She was so unhappy that she refused to eat. She just sat in a corner, pining for her old home. Hades loved her and hoped to marry her, but Persephone time and again refused, saying that she wished only to return to the world above and her mother.

Meanwhile, Demeter continued to look for her daughter from one end of the world to the other. While she searched, she gave no thought at all to the harvest. Everywhere the crops failed and the farmers watched in despair as their corn failed to ripen and their fruit withered on the trees.

Even Zeus, the King of the Gods, was worried. He did not wish to see the people on earth go hungry, so when Demeter asked him to help her find Persephone, he agreed to do what he could. His messengers soon came back with the information that she was

with Hades in the Underworld. Zeus had no power over those who lived in the Underworld but there was a chance that Persephone might be saved. She had not yet eaten anything there and so had not yet become part of the Underworld. Each day Hades' servants brought her tempting dishes of exquisite fruit and sweets, but Persephone over and over again refused to touch them because she was so unhappy.

Zeus's messengers arrived in the Underworld once more and demanded that Persephone be returned to her mother. Hades knew that unless he could make her eat he would lose the lovely girl he wanted to marry. He ordered his servants to prepare a bowl of beautiful fruit and he himself carried it to Persephone. On the top he put a sweet-smelling pomegranate which he knew was her favourite fruit. Persephone, after much coaxing, reluctantly ate six seeds from the pomegranate, for she felt Hades had been kind to her and did not want to hurt his feelings. Then she turned her head away and refused to eat any more, for the taste reminded her of the warm sunshine and the happy life that she missed so much. But Hades was triumphant, knowing that, because she had eaten food, she belonged forever to the Underworld.

Demeter was heartbroken. She grieved so much at the loss of her daughter that she had no heart to travel the earth as Goddess of the Harvest, and people began to grow hungry. Zeus was sorry

for Demeter and for the people of the earth, so he sent his messengers to Hades once more to make a bargain: Persephone should spend six months of each year in the Underworld, one for each pomegranate seed she had eaten, but for the remaining six months she should return to the earth and join her mother.

And so it has been ever since. You will know when Persephone is in the Underworld with Hades as leaves fall and plants wither and die. During the six months we call Autumn and Winter Demeter is too unhappy to give any thought to the harvest. But when Persephone returns to the earth her mother is overjoyed and in her happiness makes the flowers open and new shoots spring from the ground. Crops flourish and fruit ripens to produce food. These six months when Persephone once more dances through the fields and orchards with her mother we call Spring and Summer.

THREE BLIND MICE

Three blind mice, see how they run!
They all ran after the farmer's wife,
Who cut off their tails with a carving knife,
Did you ever see such a sight in your life,
    As three blind mice?

DAVY DUMPLING

Davy Davy Dumpling,
Boil him in the pot;
Sugar him and butter him,
And eat him while he's hot.

THE KILKENNY CATS

There once were two cats of Kilkenny,
Each thought there was one cat too many;
So they fought and they fit,
And they scratched and they bit,
   Till, excepting their nails,
   And the tips of their tails,
Instead of two cats, there weren't any.

THE CUCKOO

Cuckoo, cuckoo, what do you do?
In April I open my bill;
In May I sing all day;
In June I change my tune;
In July I prepare to fly;
In August away I must.

The Hare and the Tortoise

In the forest there was a clearing where all the animals gathered each evening after going to the river to drink. The tortoise was usually the last to arrive, and the other animals would laugh at him as he plodded into the clearing.

"Come on, Slowcoach," they would call out as he came through the grass towards them. The tortoise would blink at them and continue slowly on his way until he reached the spot where he wanted to settle down.

The liveliest of all the animals in the forest was the hare. He ran so fast that he was always the first to arrive at the clearing. "Just look at me," he was boasting one evening, "I can run faster than any of you."

The tortoise ambled into the clearing, last as usual. To everyone's surprise, he went slowly across to the hare.

"Since you run so fast, could you beat me in a race?" he asked.

"*I*, beat *you*, in a *race!*" exclaimed the hare, and he fell on the ground laughing. "Of course I would beat you. You name the distance, Tortoise, but don't make it too far for your short little legs," and he roared with laughter again.

Most of the other animals laughed too. It did seem a very comic idea. The fox said,

"Come on then, Tortoise, name the distance and the time and then we will all come to watch."

"Let us start tomorrow morning, at sunrise," suggested the

tortoise. "We'll run from this clearing to the edge of the forest and return along the bank of the river to this spot again."

"Why, it will take you all day to go so far, Tortoise. Are you sure you want to go ahead with it?" asked the hare. He grinned at the thought of the easy victory he would have.

"I am sure," replied the tortoise. "The first one back to this clearing will be the winner."

"Agreed!" said the hare, as the tortoise settled down in some long grass to sleep for the night.

The next morning the clearing was full of animals who had come to see the start of the great race. Some ran along to the edge of the forest, others chose good places to watch along the way.

The hare and the tortoise stood side by side. As the sun rose, the fox called,

"Ready, steady, go!"

The hare jumped up and in no time at all he was far ahead of the tortoise, almost out of sight. The tortoise started off in the same direction. He plodded along, slowly picking up his feet, then slowly putting them down only a little in front of where they had been before.

"Come on, Tortoise," called his friends anxiously. But he did not lift up his foot to wave at them as the hare had done. He kept on moving slowly forwards.

In a few minutes the hare was a long way from the starting line so he slowed down. "It's going to take the tortoise all day," he thought, "so there is no need for me to hurry." He stopped to talk to friends and nibble juicy grass here and there along the path.

By the time he reached half-way the sun was high in the sky and the day became very hot. The animals who were waiting there saw the hare turn back towards the clearing. They settled down for a long wait for the tortoise.

As he returned by the river, the hot sun and the grass he had eaten made the hare feel sleepy.

"There's no need to hurry," he told himself. "Here's a nice shady spot," and he stretched himself out comfortably on the ground. With paws beneath his head, he murmured sleepily, "It won't matter if Tortoise passes me, I'm much faster than he is. I'll still get back first and win the race." He drifted off to sleep.

Meanwhile the tortoise went on slowly. He reached the edge of the forest quite soon after the hare, for he had not stopped to talk to friends or eat tempting fresh grass. Before long, smiling gently, he passed the hare sleeping in the shade.

The animals in the clearing waited all day for the hare to return, but he did not arrive. The sun was setting before they saw the tortoise plodding towards them.

"Where is the hare?" they called out. The tortoise did not waste his breath in answering but came steadily towards them.

"Hurrah, Tortoise has won. Well done, Slowcoach!" the animals cheered.

Only when he knew he had won the race did Tortoise speak.

"Hare? Oh, he's asleep back there by the river."

There was a sudden flurry and at great speed the hare burst into the clearing. He had woken and, seeing how long the shadows were, realized he had slept for much longer than he intended. He raced back to the clearing but he was too late.

Tortoise smiled and said, "Slow and steady wins the race."

DAYS IN THE MONTHS

Thirty days hath September,
April, June, and November;
All the rest have thirty-one.
Excepting February alone,
And that has twenty-eight days clear
And twenty-nine in each leap year.

A MAN IN THE WILDERNESS

A man in the wilderness asked of me,
How many strawberries grow in the sea?
I answered him, as I thought good,
As many as red herrings swim in the wood.

PAT-A-CAKE

Pat-a-cake, pat-a-cake, baker's man,
Bake me a cake as fast as you can;
Pat it and prick it, and mark it with B,
Put it in the oven for Baby and me.

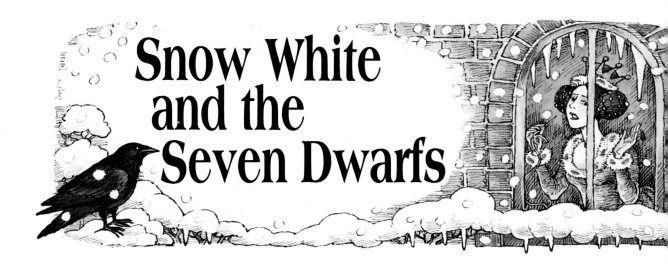

Snow White and the Seven Dwarfs

One winter a beautiful queen sat sewing by a window. As she gazed down at the snow-covered garden she saw a black raven and, at the same moment, she happened to prick her finger on her needle – a drop of blood fell on the snow. The colours were so strong that the queen said to herself, "If only I could have a child whose skin was as white as snow, with hair as black as a raven and lips as red as blood."

Not long afterwards the queen had a baby daughter, and when she saw her jet black hair, snowy white skin and red lips she remembered her strange wish on that winter's day and named her Snow White.

But after a few years Snow White's mother died and her father married again. The new queen, Snow White's stepmother, was beautiful too, but she was also proud and vain. She had a magic mirror and each day she would admire herself in it and ask,

"Mirror, mirror, on the wall,
Who is the fairest one of all?"
and the mirror would always reply,
"You, O Queen, are the fairest one of all."

The queen would smile when she heard this for she knew the mirror always spoke the truth. As the years went by, Snow White grew prettier and prettier, until one day, when the queen looked in the magic mirror, the mirror replied,

"You, O Queen, are fair, 'tis true,
But Snow White is fairer now than you."

The queen was filled with envy. From that day on she hated Snow White. Finally she called for a hunter and told him to take Snow White deep into the forest and kill her.

"Cut out her heart and bring it back to me to prove she is dead," she commanded.

The hunter felt very sad. Like everyone in the king's household he loved Snow White, but he knew he must obey the queen's orders. He took Snow White deep into the forest and pulled out his knife. Snow White fell to her knees in terror. The hunter took pity on her and told her to hide. Then he killed a deer and cut out its heart to take back to the cruel queen.

On her own in the forest, Snow White felt afraid. She began to run here and there through the trees, but she did not know which way to go. In the evening she came to a clearing and found a little house. She wondered if it was a woodman's cottage where she might be able to stay. When she knocked at the door, there was no answer.

Snow White lifted the latch and went inside. There she saw a room all neat and tidy with a little table laid with seven places — seven little knives and forks, seven little wooden plates and drinking cups. Snow White was hungry and thirsty so she ate some food from each plate and drank a drop from each cup. She did not want to empty one person's plate and cup only.

Beyond the table were seven little beds all neatly made. Snow White tried them all out and the seventh bed was just right. She lay down and fell into a deep sleep, exhausted by her long journey through the forest.

The cottage was the home of seven dwarfs. All day long they worked in a mine nearby, digging diamonds from deep inside the mountain. When they returned home that night, they were startled to see that someone had entered their cottage and had taken some food and drink from each place at their table. They were even more surprised to find their beds disturbed. When the seventh dwarf found Snow White in his bed he called to the others. They all gathered around her and marvelled at her beauty. Being kind little men they decided not to disturb her.

When Snow White awoke the next day she told the dwarfs her story. "I have no home now," she said sadly, and at once the dwarfs asked her to stay with them in the cottage. Snow White agreed happily, and each morning when the dwarfs went off to work, she stayed behind and kept their cottage clean and cooked their supper.

At the palace the queen welcomed the hunter when he returned with the deer's heart. She was certain that once again she was the most beautiful woman in the world. As soon as she was alone she looked in her magic mirror and said,

"Mirror, mirror, on the wall,
Who is the fairest one of all?"

To her horror, the mirror replied,

"You, O Queen, are fair, 'tis true,
But Snow White is fairer still than you."

The queen trembled with rage as she realized that the hunter had tricked her. She decided that she would seek out Snow White and kill her herself.

The queen disguised herself as an old pedlar woman with a tray of ribbons and pretty things to sell and she set off into the forest. When she came to the dwarfs' cottage she knocked and cried out, "Pretty goods for sale! Pretty goods for sale!"

Snow White came to the door and looked eagerly at the tray. The queen noticed that she was attracted by some lacing ribbons and asked if Snow White would like to try one on. Snow White nodded, so the queen threaded a ribbon through her bodice. Then she tugged the lacing so tight that Snow White could not breathe and fell to the ground. The queen hurried back to the palace sure that this time Snow White was truly dead.

When the dwarfs returned that evening, they found Snow White lying on the floor, deathly cold and still. They gathered around her in dismay. Then they noticed that she had a new lacing on her dress which had been tied too tightly. Quickly they cut it open and Snow White started breathing again.

All seven dwarfs gave a tremendous sigh of relief as by now they loved Snow White dearly. She told them what had happened. The dwarfs suspected that the old pedlar woman was Snow White's wicked stepmother and that she would try to harm Snow White again if she ever found out that she was still alive. They begged her not to allow anyone into the cottage while she was alone and told her not to buy anything from strangers.

At the palace the queen smiled at her reflection in the magic mirror and asked,

> "Mirror, mirror, on the wall,
> Who is the fairest one of all?"

and the mirror replied,

> "You, O Queen, are fair, 'tis true,
> But Snow White is fairer still than you."

The queen was speechless with rage. She realized that yet again her plan to kill Snow White had failed. She resolved to try again and this time she was determined to succeed. She chose an apple with one rosy-red side and one yellow side. Carefully she injected poison into the red part of the apple and carefully she placed it in a basket of apples, on the very top.

The wicked queen, disguised this time as a peasant woman, set out once more into the forest. Once more she knocked at the dwarfs' cottage. She knew that Snow White would be wary by now so she simply chatted to her and, as Snow White became less nervous, she offered her an apple as a present. Snow White was tempted as the rosy apple looked delicious but she refused, explaining that she had been told not to accept anything from strangers.

"I will show you how harmless it is," said the disguised queen. "I will take a bite first and if I am unharmed you will know that it is safe."

The queen had not poisoned the yellow side of the apple so she took a bite from there. When nothing happened, Snow White stretched out her hand for the apple. She too took a bite, but from the rosy-red side. Instantly the poison attacked Snow White and she fell down as though dead. The triumphant queen cackled with glee as she returned to the palace.

When the dwarfs found Snow White that evening they could not revive her. All night they watched over her, but when morning came and still she did not move or speak, they decided she must be dead.

Weeping bitterly, the dwarfs laid her in a coffin and placed a glass lid over the top so that all could admire her beauty even though she was dead. Then they carried the coffin to the top of a hill where night and day they stood guard over their beautiful Snow White.

The wicked queen was delighted that day when she looked in her mirror and asked,

"Mirror, mirror, on the wall,
Who is the fairest one of all?"
and the mirror replied,

"You, O Queen, are the fairest one of all."
She gave a cruel laugh when she heard those words. They meant that her plan to kill Snow White had at last succeeded.

As the years passed, the story of Snow White's beauty spread far and wide. One day a prince came to see the coffin for himself. Snow White looked so lovely that he fell in love with her at once and asked the dwarfs to allow him to take the coffin with him back to his own country. The dwarfs loved Snow White too much to permit him to do this, but they agreed to let him kiss her.

As the prince gently raised Snow White's head to kiss her, the piece of poisoned apple fell from her lips and she stirred a little. She was alive.

"Where am I?" she asked, looking at the prince.

"Safe with me," replied the prince, and Snow White too fell in love.

At that moment, the wicked queen was looking in her mirror and the mirror said,

"You, O Queen, are fair 'tis true,
But Snow White is fairer still than you."

The queen cursed Snow White in fury. But by now the king had discovered what evil deeds the queen had planned and he banished her from his kingdom. That night she left the palace and no one ever saw her or her mirror again.

Snow White said farewell to her kind friends, the seven dwarfs, and rode away with her prince. They were married at his father's castle and lived for a long time afterwards in happiness and peace.

JACK AND JILL

Jack and Jill
Went up the hill,
To fetch a pail of water;
Jack fell down,
And broke his crown,
And Jill came tumbling after.

Then up Jack got,
And home did trot,
As fast as he could caper;
To old Dame Dob,
Who patched his nob
With vinegar and brown paper.

When Jill came in,
How she did grin
To see Jack's paper plaster;
His mother, vexed,
Did whip her next,
For laughing at Jack's disaster.

Now Jack did laugh
And Jill did cry,
But her tears did soon abate;
Then Jill did say,
That they should play
At see-saw across the gate.

The Little Jackal

There was once a little jackal who lived in the jungle. He was a greedy little jackal, and one of his favourite meals was fresh crabs from the river. One day he went down to the big river near his home and put his paw in the water to pull out a crab.

Snap! A large, lazy crocodile who had been lying in the water snapped his jaws and caught the jackal's paw. The little jackal did not cry out, although he was very frightened. Instead he laughed.

"Ha! Ha! That crocodile in the river thinks he has caught my paw, but the stupid animal does not realize he has snapped up a piece of wood and is holding it in his jaws."

The crocodile immediately opened his mouth for he did not want to be seen with a log of wood in his jaws. Quickly the little jackal danced away and called cheekily from a safe distance:

"I'll catch some crabs another day, Mr Crocodile."

The crocodile lashed his tail with rage and resolved to catch the little jackal and eat him the next time he came to the river.

A week later, when his paw was healed, the jackal came back to the river to catch crabs. He did not want to be eaten by the crocodile, so he called out from a safe distance:

"I can't see any crabs lying on the bank. I'll have to dip my paw into the water near the edge," and he watched the river for a few minutes.

The crocodile thought, "Now is my chance to catch the jackal," and he swam close to the river bank.

When the little jackal saw the water move, he called out:

"Thank you, Mr Crocodile. Now I know you are there, I'll come back another day."

The crocodile lashed his tail with rage until he stirred up the mud from the bottom of the river. He swore he would not let the little jackal trick him again.

The jackal could not stop thinking about the crabs, so a few days later he went down to the river again. He could not see the crocodile so he called out:

"I know crabs make bubbles in the water, so as soon as I see bubbles I'll dip my paw in and then I'll catch them easily."

When he heard this, the crocodile, who was lying just beneath the water started to blow bubbles as fast as he could. He was sure that the jackal would put his paw in where the bubbles were rising and *Snap!* This time he would have the little jackal.

But when the jackal saw the bubbles, he called out:

"Thank you, Mr Crocodile, for showing me where you are. I'll come back another day for the crabs."

The crocodile was so angry at being tricked again that he waited till the jackal's back was turned, then he jumped out of the river and followed the jackal, determined to catch him and eat him this time.

Now the jackal, who was very hungry, made his way to the fig grove to eat some figs. By the time the crocodile arrived, he was having a lovely feast munching the ripe blue fruit, and licking his lips with pleasure.

The crocodile was exhausted by walking on land which he found was much more difficult than swimming in the river. "I am too tired to catch the jackal now," he said to himself. "But I'll set a trap and catch him next time he comes for the figs."

The next day, the greedy jackal returned to the fig grove. He did love eating figs! To his surprise he saw a large and rather untidy pile of figs that had not been there before. "I wonder if my friend the crocodile has anything to do with this?" he said to himself, and he called out:

"What a lovely pile of figs! All I need to do is to see which figs wave in the breeze, for it is always the ripest and most delicious figs that wave in the breeze. I shall then know which ones to eat."

Of course the crocodile was buried under the pile of figs and when he heard this he smiled a big toothy crocodile smile. "All I have to do is to wriggle a bit," he thought. "When the jackal sees the figs move he will come and eat them and this time I will certainly catch him."

The little jackal watched as the crocodile wriggled under the pile of figs, and he laughed and laughed.

"Thank you, Mr Crocodile," he said, "I'll come back another day when you are not here."

Now the crocodile was really in a rage so he followed the little jackal to his house to catch him there. There was no one at home when the crocodile got there, but the crocodile thought, "I will wait here, and catch him when he comes home tonight."

He was too big to go through the gate, so he broke it and then he was too big to go through the door, so he smashed that. "Never mind," he said to himself. "I will eat the little jackal tonight whatever happens," and he lay in wait for the jackal in the jackal's little house.

When the jackal came home he saw the broken gate, and smashed door, and he said to himself, "I wonder if my friend the crocodile has anything to do with this?"

"Little house," he called out, "why haven't you said 'hello' to me as you do each night when I come home?"

The crocodile heard this, and thought he ought to make everything seem as normal as possible, so he shouted out:

"Hello little jackal!"

Then a wicked smile appeared on the jackal's face. He fetched some twigs and branches, piled them up outside his house, and set fire to it. As the house burned he called out:

"A roast crocodile is safer than a live crocodile! I shall go and build myself a new house by the river where I can catch all the crabs I want."

With that he skipped off to the river bank and for all I know he is still there today, eating crabs all day long, and laughing at the way he tricked the crocodile.

HODDLEY, PODDLEY

Hoddley, poddley, puddle and fogs,
Cats are to marry the poodle dogs;
Cats in blue jackets and dogs in red hats,
What will become of the mice and the rats?

LITTLE BO-PEEP

Little Bo-peep has lost her sheep,
  And can't tell where to find them;
Leave them alone, and they'll come home,
  Bringing their tails behind them.

Little Bo-peep fell fast asleep,
  And dreamt she heard them bleating;
But when she awoke, she found it a joke,
  For they were still a-fleeting.

Then up she took her little crook,
    Determined for to find them;
She found them indeed, but it made her heart bleed
    For they'd left their tails behind them.

It happened one day, as Bo-peep did stray
    Into a meadow hard by,
There she espied their tails side by side,
    All hung on a tree to dry.

She heaved a sigh, and wiped her eye,
    And over the hillocks went rambling,
And tried what she could as a shepherdess should,
    To tack each again to its lambkin.

Rapunzel

Along time ago, a husband and wife lived happily in a cottage at the edge of a wood. But one day the wife fell ill. She could eat nothing and grew thinner and thinner. The only thing that could cure her, she believed, was a strange herb that grew in the beautiful garden next to their cottage. She begged her husband to find a way into the garden and steal some of this herb, which was called rapunzel.

Now this garden belonged to a wicked witch, who used it to grow herbs for her spells. One day, she caught the husband creeping into her garden. When he told her what he had come for, the witch gave him some rapunzel, but she made him promise to give her their first-born child in return. The husband agreed, thinking that the witch would soon forget the promise. He took the rapunzel back to the cottage and gave it to his wife. As soon as she had eaten it she felt better.

A year later, a baby girl was born and the witch *did* come and take her away. She told the couple they would be able to see their

daughter in the garden behind their house. Over the years they were able to watch her grow up into a beautiful child, with long fair hair. The witch called her Rapunzel after the plant her father had come to take.

When she was twelve years old, the witch decided to lock Rapunzel up in a high tower in case she tried to run away. The tower had no door or staircase, but Rapunzel was quite happy up there as she could sit at the window watching the life of the forest and talking to the birds. Yet sometimes she would sigh, for she longed to be back in the beautiful garden where she could play in the sunshine. Then she would sing to cheer herself up.

Each day, the witch came to see her, bringing her fresh food. She would stand at the bottom of the tower and call out,

"Rapunzel, Rapunzel, let down your long hair."

Rapunzel, whose long golden hair was plaited, would twist it round one of the bars and drop it out of the window, and the witch would climb up it. When she left, Rapunzel would let down her golden hair again, and the witch would slide nimbly down.

One day, the king's son was riding through the forest when he heard Rapunzel singing. Mystified, he rode to the tower, but could see no door, so could not understand how anyone could be there. He decided to stay and watch the tower and listen to the singing. After a while the witch came along and the prince watched her carefully as she stood at the bottom of the tower and called out,

"Rapunzel, Rapunzel, let down your long hair."

To the prince's amazement, a long golden plait of hair fell almost to the ground. When he saw the witch climb up the hair and disappear through the window, he made up his mind he would wait until she had gone and see if he could do the same.

So after the witch had gone, he stood where the witch had been and called,

"Rapunzel, Rapunzel, let down your long hair."

When the golden plait came tumbling down, he climbed up as the witch had done and found to his astonishment the most beautiful girl he had ever seen. They talked for a long time and then the prince left, promising to come again. Rapunzel looked forward to his visits, for she had been lonely. He told her all about the world outside her tower, and they fell deeply in love.

One day Rapunzel said to the witch, "Why is it when you climb up my hair you are so heavy? The handsome prince who comes is much lighter than you." At this, the witch flew into a rage. She took Rapunzel out of the tower and led her deep into the forest to a lonely spot, and told her she must stay there without food or shelter. The witch cut off Rapunzel's long plait of golden hair and then hurried back to the tower.

That evening when the prince came by, he called out as usual, "Rapunzel, Rapunzel, let down your long hair."

The witch, who had fastened the plait of golden hair inside the window, threw it down. The prince climbed up eagerly, only to be confronted with the wicked witch. "Aha," she cackled, "so you

are the visitor who has been coming to see my little Rapunzel. I will make sure you won't ever see her again," and she tried to scratch out his eyes.

The prince jumped out of the high window and landed in a clump of thorny bushes. His face, however, was badly scratched and his eyes hurt so much that he could not see, and he stumbled off blindly into the forest.

After several days of wandering and suffering, he heard somebody singing. Following the sound, he drew closer and realized he had found Rapunzel, who was singing as she worked to make a home for herself in the forest. He ran towards her, calling her name, and she came and kissed him. As she did so, his eyes were healed and he could see again.

The prince took Rapunzel to his father's palace, where he told their story. She was reunited with her parents, and then a grand wedding took place. Rapunzel married the prince and lived with him happily for many years. As for the witch, a royal proclamation banished her from the kingdom and she was never seen again.

JACK SPRAT

Jack Sprat could eat no fat,
   His wife could eat no lean,
And so between them both, you see,
   They licked the platter clean.

DOCTOR FOSTER

Doctor Foster went to Gloucester
In a shower of rain;
   He stepped in a puddle,
   Right up to his middle,
And never went there again.

YANKEE DOODLE

Yankee Doodle came to town,
   Riding on a pony,
He stuck a feather in his cap
   And called it macaroni.

TO THE RAIN

Rain, rain, go away,
Come again another day,
Little Johnny wants to play.
Rain, rain, go to Spain,
Never show your face again.

STAR LIGHT

Star light, star bright,
First star I see tonight,
I wish I may, I wish I might,
Have the wish I wish tonight.

JACK HORNER

Little Jack Horner
Sat in the corner,
Eating his Christmas pie;
He put in his thumb,
And pulled out a plum,
And said, What a good boy am I!

The Little Red Hen

Once upon a time there was a little red hen. She lived with a pig, a duck and a cat. They all lived in a house which the little red hen kept clean and tidy. The others never helped. Although they said they meant to, they were all far too lazy. The pig liked to grunt in the mud outside, the duck used to swim in the pond all day, and the cat enjoyed lying in the sun, purring.

One day the little red hen found a grain of corn.

"Who will plant this grain of corn?" she asked.

"Not I," grunted the pig from his muddy patch in the garden.

"Not I," quacked the duck from her pond.

"Not I," purred the cat from his place in the sun.

So the little red hen found a nice bit of earth, scratched it with her feet and planted the grain of corn herself.

During the summer the grain of corn grew. First it grew into a tall green stalk, then it ripened in the sun until it had turned a lovely golden colour.

"Who will help me cut the corn?" asked the little red hen.

"Not I," grunted the pig from his muddy patch in the garden.

"Not I," quacked the duck from her pond.

"Not I," purred the cat from his place in the sun.

"Very well then, I shall cut it myself," said the little red hen. Carefully she cut the stalk and took out all the grains of corn from the husks.

"Who will take the corn to the mill, so that it can be ground into flour?" asked the little red hen.

"Not I," grunted the pig from his muddy patch in the garden.

"Not I," quacked the duck from her pond.

"Not I," purred the cat from his place in the sun.

"Very well, I shall take it myself." said the little red hen.

So the little red hen took the corn to the mill herself, and asked the miller to grind it into flour.

In time the miller sent a little bag of flour down to the house where the little red hen lived with the pig, the duck and the cat.

"Who will help me to make the flour into bread?" asked the little red hen.

"Not I," grunted the pig from his muddy patch in the garden.

"Not I," quacked the duck from her pond.

"Not I," purred the cat from his place in the sun.

"Very well," said the little red hen. "I shall make the bread myself."

She mixed the flour into dough. She kneaded the dough and put it into the oven to bake.

Soon there was a lovely smell of hot fresh bread. It filled all the corners of the house and wafted out into the garden. The pig came into the kitchen from his muddy patch in the garden, the duck came in from the pond and the cat left his place in the sun. When the little red hen opened the oven door the dough had risen and turned into the most delicious-looking loaf.

"Who is going to eat this bread?" asked the little red hen.

"I will," grunted the pig.

"I will," quacked the duck.

"I will," purred the cat.

"Oh no, you won't," said the little red hen. "I planted the seed, I cut the corn, I took it to the mill to be made into flour, and I made the bread, all by myself. I shall eat it all by myself."

The pig, the duck and the cat all stood and watched as the little red hen ate the loaf all by herself. It was delicious and she enjoyed it, right to the very last crumb.

ONE, TWO

1, 2,
Buckle my shoe;

3, 4,
Knock at the door;

5, 6,
Pick up sticks;

7, 8,
Lay them straight;

9, 10,
A big fat hen;

11, 12
Dig and delve;

13, 14,
Maids a-courting;

17, 18,
Maids a-waiting;

15, 16,
Maids in the kitchen;

19, 20,
My plate's empty.

Little Red Riding Hood

There was once a pretty little girl who lived in a cottage on the edge of a wood. Her grandmother, who lived at the other side of the wood, had made her a warm red cape with a hood and, as she often wore it, she became known as Little Red Riding Hood.

One day her mother called her and said, "Little Red Riding Hood, will you take this basket of food to your grandmother? She isn't very well. Carry the basket carefully for I have filled it with some cakes, some fresh bread and some butter."

Little Red Riding Hood put on her red cape and, carrying the basket carefully, she set off through the wood to her grandmother's cottage. By and by she wandered off the path to pick some flowers. Then, quite unexpectedly, she met a wolf. He could have eaten her there and then, but he could hear some woodcutters working close by.

"Where are you going, little girl?" he asked instead.

"I'm going to my grandmother," Little Red Riding Hood answered. "She is ill and I have a basket of food for her."

"And where does your grandmother live?" asked the wolf, thinking if he was clever he might be able to eat the little girl *and* her grandmother.

"Through the wood and hers is the first cottage you can see," replied Little Red Riding Hood. She went on slowly through the wood, stopping here and there to add some more flowers to the bunch she was holding. The wolf watched her go and then he ran through the trees to the grandmother's cottage.

He knocked at the door.

"Who is there?" he heard the old lady call.

Making his voice sound as much like Little Red Riding Hood's as he could, the wicked wolf answered, "It's me, Grandmother. It's Little Red Riding Hood with some presents for you."

"Pull the bobbin and the latch will go up," called the old lady from her bed.

The wolf pulled the bobbin, the latch went up, and he bounded into the room. In a trice he had gobbled up the poor old lady. He put on her shawl and nightcap and got into her bed to wait for Little Red Riding Hood.

In a while there was a knock at the door.

Trying to make his voice sound as much like the old lady's as possible, the wolf quavered, "Who is there?"

"It's me, Little Red Riding Hood," answered the girl. "I have brought you some food from my mother."

"Pull the bobbin and the latch will go up," called the wolf.

The voice sounded rather gruff to Little Red Riding Hood. She thought her grandmother must have a sore throat. The wolf tugged the bedclothes up under his chin as Little Red Riding Hood pulled the bobbin and walked into the cottage.

Although she saw someone in the bed wearing a shawl and nightcap, Little Red Riding Hood was rather puzzled. Her grandmother seemed quite different.

"What big eyes you have, Grandmother!" she said.

"All the better to see you with!" said the wolf.

"What big ears you have, Grandmother!"

"All the better to hear you with!" said the wolf.

"What big teeth you have, Grandmother!"

"All the better to eat you with!" said the wolf and he sprang out of bed.

Little Red Riding Hood screamed with fright. Luckily the woodcutters were passing by and heard her screams. They rushed inside and killed the wolf instantly. Out jumped the old lady, alive and well but feeling rather shaken by her adventure. She was delighted to see Little Red Riding Hood and her basket of food.

Little Red Riding Hood took care never to talk to wolves again, and she always stayed on the path whenever she went through the wood to visit her grandmother.

HICKORY, DICKORY, DOCK

Hickory, dickory, dock,
The mouse ran up the clock.
   The clock struck one,
   The mouse ran down,
Hickory, dickory, dock.

THE MISCHIEVOUS RAVEN

A farmer went trotting upon his grey mare,
   Bumpety, bumpety, bump!
With his daughter behind him so rosy and fair,
   Lumpety, lumpety, lump!

A raven cried, Croak! and they all tumbled down,
   Bumpety, bumpety, bump!
The mare broke her knees and the farmer his crown,
   Lumpety, lumpety, lump!

The mischievous raven flew laughing away,
   Bumpety, bumpety, bump!
And vowed he would serve them the same the next day,
   Lumpety, lumpety, lump!

The Three Little Pigs

Once upon a time there were three little pigs. One day they set out from the farm where they had been born. They were going out into the world to make their fortune.

The first little pig met a man carrying some straw, and he asked him if he might have some to build himself a house.

"Of course, little pig," said the man. He gave the little pig a big bundle of straw, and the little pig built himself a lovely little house of golden straw.

By and by a big bad wolf came along and saw the new house. Feeling rather hungry and thinking he would like to eat a little pig for supper, he called out,

"Little pig, little pig, let me come in."
To which the little pig replied,

"No, no, by the hair of my chinny chin chin,
I'll not let you in."
So the wolf shouted crossly,

"Then I'll huff and I'll puff,
Till I blow your house in!"
And he huffed and he puffed until the house of straw fell in, and he ate the little pig for supper.

The second little pig was walking along the road when he met a man with a bundle of sticks. "Please, Sir," he said, "can you let me have some of those sticks so that I can build a house?"

"Of course," said the man, and he gave him a big pile of sticks. In no time at all, the little pig had built himself a lovely little house of sticks.

By and by along came the same big bad wolf. When he saw another little pig, this time in a wooden house, he called out,

"Little pig, little pig, let me come in."

To which the little pig replied,

"No, no, by the hair of my chinny chin chin,
I'll not let you in."

So the wolf shouted,

"Then I'll huff and I'll puff,
Till I blow your house in!"

And he huffed and he puffed and he huffed and he puffed until the house of sticks fell in, and he gobbled up the little pig.

The third little pig met a man with a cartload of bricks. "Please, Sir, can I have some bricks to build myself a house?" he asked, and when the man had given him some, he built himself a lovely little brick house.

By and by the big bad wolf came along, and licked his lips as
he thought about the third little pig. He called out,
    "Little pig, little pig, let me come in."
And the little pig replied,
    "No, no, by the hair of my chinny chin chin,
    I'll not let you in."

So the wolf shouted,

"Then I'll huff and I'll puff,
Till I blow your house in!"

And the wolf huffed and he puffed, and he huffed and he puffed, and he HUFFED again and he PUFFED again, but still the house, which had been so well built with bricks, did not fall in.

The wolf went away to think how he could trick the little pig. He came back and called through the window of the brick house,

"Little pig, there are some juicy turnips in the farmer's field. Shall we go there tomorrow morning at six o'clock and get some?"

The little pig thought this was a good idea, as he was fond of turnips, but he went at five o'clock, not six o'clock, and collected all the turnips he needed before the wolf arrived.

The wolf was furious, but he soon thought of another trick. He told the little pig about the apples in the farmer's orchard, and suggested they both went to get some at five o'clock the next morning. The little pig agreed, and went, as before, an hour earlier. But this time the wolf came early too and arrived while the little pig was still in the apple tree. The little pig pretended to be pleased to see him and threw an apple down to the wolf. While the wolf was picking it up, the little pig jumped down from the tree and got into a barrel. He rolled quickly down the hill inside this barrel and rushed into his house of bricks.

The wolf was furious that the little pig had got the better of him again, and chased him in the barrel back to his house. When he got there, he climbed onto the roof, intending to come down the chimney and catch the little pig that way. But the little pig was waiting for him with a large cauldron of boiling water on the fire. The wolf came down the chimney and fell into the cauldron with a big SPLASH, and the little pig quickly put the lid on it.

The wicked wolf was never seen again, and the little pig lived happily in his house of bricks for many years.

POP GOES THE WEASEL!

Up and down the City Road,
　In and out the Eagle,
That's the way the money goes,
　Pop goes the weasel!

Half a pound of tuppeny rice,
　Half a pound of treacle,
Mix it up and make it nice,
　Pop goes the weasel!

Every night when I go out
　The monkey's on the table;
Take a stick and knock it off,
　Pop goes the weasel!

JEREMIAH

Jeremiah, blow the fire,
　Puff, puff, puff!
First you blow it gently,
　Then you blow it rough.

SOLOMON GRUNDY

Solomon Grundy,
Born on a Monday,
Christened on Tuesday,
Married on Wednesday,
Took ill on Thursday,
Worse on Friday,
Died on Saturday,
Buried on Sunday.
This is the end
Of Solomon Grundy.

Rumpelstiltskin

One day a king was riding through a village in his kingdom when he heard a woman singing.

"My daughter has burnt five cakes today,
My daughter has burnt five cakes today."

It was the miller's wife who was cross with her daughter for being so careless. The king stopped to hear her song again. The miller's wife hoped to impress the king so she sang,

"My daughter has spun fine gold today,
My daughter has spun fine gold today."

And she boasted that her daughter could spin straw into gold.

The king was greatly impressed and said to the miller's wife,

"If your daughter will spin for me in my palace, I'll give her many presents. I might even make her my queen."

"What a wonderful opportunity," thought the miller's wife, and she fetched her daughter.

The king took the girl back to the palace. He ordered a spinning wheel to be placed in a room filled with straw.

"Spin this into gold by the morning or you will die," he commanded, and he locked her in.

The poor girl wept bitterly. For of course she could not spin straw into gold as her mother had foolishly boasted.

Suddenly a little man appeared from nowhere.

"What will you give me, pretty girl, if I spin this straw into gold for you?" he asked.

"My necklace," said the girl.

The little man sat down by the spinning wheel. Singing strange songs, he spun all the straw into fine gold thread. Then he

took the girl's necklace and, with a skip and a hop and a stamp of his foot, he disappeared .

When the king unlocked the room the next morning he was delighted to see the skeins of golden thread. But that evening he took the miller's daughter to another room with an even bigger pile of straw.

"Spin this into gold by the morning," he ordered, "or you will die." And out he went, locking the door behind him.

The poor girl stared at the straw and the spinning wheel. Suddenly the same little man stood before her.

"What will you give me this time if I spin your gold for you?"

"My bracelet," said the miller's daughter.

The little man set the spinning wheel whirring. Singing his strange songs, he quickly turned the straw into gold thread. By dawn he had finished and, snatching the bracelet, he disappeared with a skip and a hop and a stamp of his foot.

The king was delighted that morning, but still not satisfied. "If this girl can really spin gold from straw," he thought to himself greedily, "I shall always be rich if I make her my wife and keep her here. I shall try her once more."

So on the third night the king took the miller's daughter into another room with an even greater pile of straw.

"Spin this into gold," he commanded. "If you succeed, I shall marry you and you shall be queen. If you fail, I shall chop off your head." And out he went, locking the door behind him.

Once more, as the girl wept bitterly before the pile of straw and the spinning wheel, the little man appeared from nowhere.

"I see you need my help again," he said. "How will you reward me this time if I save your life?"

"I have nothing more to give you," the miller's daughter said in despair.

"Ah!" said the little man, "but if the straw is spun into gold tonight, you will become queen. Will you promise to give me your first child when it is born?"

"Yes! Yes!" cried the girl. She was sure that when this time came she could somehow save her child.

So the little man sat and twirled the spinning wheel, tap-tapping his foot on the floor and singing his strange songs. Then, with a skip and a hop and a stamp of his foot, he was gone.

The next day the king was delighted with the gold, and he made the miller's daughter his queen as he had promised.

And as queen the miller's daughter forgot all about her promise to the little man. About a year later, a fine son was born, and she was horrified when the little man appeared again.

"I have come to claim the child you promised me," he said, stamping his foot as he spoke.

"Take my jewels and all this gold," pleaded the queen, "only leave me my little son."

The little man thought for a moment and said, "Very well, I will give you three days in which to guess my name. You may have three guesses each night. If you fail, the baby is mine."

The queen sent for all her servants and asked them to go throughout the kingdom asking if anyone had heard of the little man and if they knew his name. The first night the little man came the queen tried some unusual names.

"Is it Caspar?" she asked.

"No!" he said and stamped his foot in delight.

"Is it Balthazar?"

"No!" he said and stamped his foot again.

"Is it Melchior?"

"No!" he cried. He stamped his foot and disappeared.

The next evening the queen thought she would try some everyday names. So when the little man appeared she asked,

"Is your name John?"

"No!" he said with his usual stamp.

"Is it Michael?"

"Is it James?"

"No! No!" he cried, stamping his foot each time, and again he disappeared.

On the third and final day the queen was distraught for she could not see how she could guess the little man's name.

The palace servants came back without any news, all except for one who returned to the palace towards the end of the day. He went straight to the queen and told her that at the very edge of the kingdom, under the mountains, he had heard a little man singing this strange song as he danced around his fire:

"Today I brew, tomorrow I bake,
Next day the queen's child I'll take.
How glad I am that nobody knows
My name is Rumpelstiltskin."

The queen clapped her hands with joy and rewarded the servant for his discovery. That night the little man appeared and asked if she had guessed his name.

"Is it Ichabod?"

"No!" he cried with pleasure as he stamped his foot.

"Is it Carl?"

"No!" he shouted and stamped his foot with glee.

"Is it..." the queen hesitated. "Is it Rumpelstiltskin?"

Now it was the queen's turn to laugh. The little man stamped his foot so hard it went right through the floor and that was the end of Rumpelstiltskin.

TO MARKET

To market, to market, to buy a fat pig,
Home again, home again, jiggety-jig;

To market, to market, to buy a fat hog,
Home again, home again, jiggety-jog.

IPSEY WIPSEY

Ipsey Wipsey spider,
   Went up the garden spout;
Down came the rain
   And washed the spider out;
Out came the sun
   And dried up all the rain;
Ipsey Wipsey spider,
   Went up the spout again.

GOOSE FEATHERS

Cackle, cackle, Mother Goose,
Have you any feathers loose?
Truly have I, pretty fellow,
Half enough to fill a pillow.
Here are quills, take one or two,
And down to make a bed for you.

TO THE SNAIL

Snail, snail, put out your horns,
And I'll give you bread and barley corns.

115

Brer Rabbit's New House

Long ago an old man called Uncle Remus used to tell stories to a little boy. The two of them lived on a plantation in the southern states of America, and the stories were always about certain animals, Brer Rabbit and Brer Fox in particular, but several others too, Brer Bear and Brer Possum for instance. All too often Brer Rabbit, who was an impudent scoundrel, came out best, although he was one of the smaller creatures. Of course, to do this he had to use his wits.

One evening, Uncle Remus ate his supper as usual and then looked at the child over his spectacles.

"Now then, honey," he said. "Let's see if I can call to mind how old Brer Rabbit got himself a two-storey house without paying much for it."

He paused a moment. Then he began:

It turned out one time that a whole lot of creatures decided to build a house together. Old Brer Bear, he was among them, and Brer Fox and Brer Wolf and Brer Coon and Brer Possum, and possibly Brer Mink too. Anyway, there was a whole bunch of them, and they set to work and built a house in less than no time.

Brer Rabbit, he pretended it made his head swim to climb the scaffolding, and that it made him feel dizzy to work in the sun, but he got a board, and he stuck a pencil behind his ear, and he went round measuring and marking, measuring and marking.

He looked so busy that all the other creatures were sure he was doing the most work, and folks going along the road said, "My, my, that Brer Rabbit is doing more work than the whole lot of them put together." Yet all the time Brer Rabbit was doing nothing, and he had plenty of time to lie in the shade.

Meanwhile, the other creatures, they built the house, and it sure was a fine one. It had an upstairs and a downstairs, and chimneys all round, and it had rooms for all the creatures who had helped to make it.

Brer Rabbit, he picked out one of the upstairs rooms, and he got a gun and a brass cannon, and when no one was looking he put them up in the room. Then he got a big bowl of dirty water and carried it up there when no one was looking.

When the house was finished and all the animals were sitting in the parlour after supper, Brer Rabbit, he got up and stretched himself, and made excuses, saying he believed he'd go to his room. When he got there, and while all the others were laughing and chatting and being sociable downstairs, Brer Rabbit stuck his head out of the room and hollered.

"When a big man wants to sit down, whereabouts is he going to sit?" says he.

The other creatures laughed, and called back, 'If a big man like you can't sit in a chair he'd better sit on the floor."

"Watch out, down there," says old Brer Rabbit, "because I'm going to sit down," says he.

With that, *bang!* went Brer Rabbit's gun. The other creatures looked round at one another in astonishment as much as to say, "What in the name of gracious is that?"

They listened and listened, but they didn't hear any more fuss and it wasn't long before they were all chatting and talking again.

Then Brer Rabbit stuck his head out of his room again, and hollered, "When a big man like me wants to sneeze, whereabouts is he going to sneeze?"

The other creatures called back, "A big man like you can sneeze anywhere he wants."

"Watch out down there, then," says Brer Rabbit, "because I'm going to sneeze right here," says he.

With that Brer Rabbit let off his cannon – *bulder-um-m-m!* The window panes rattled. The whole house shook as though it would come down, and old Brer Bear fell out of his rocking chair – *kerblump!*

When they all settled down again Brer Possum and Brer Mink suggested that as Brer Rabbit had such a bad cold they would step outside and get some fresh air. The other creatures said that they would stick it out, and before long they all got their hair smoothed down and began to talk again.

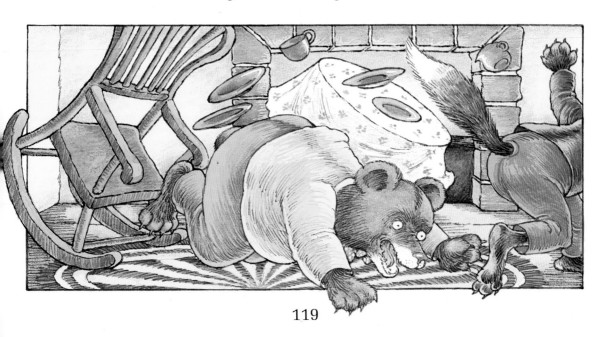

After a while, when they were beginning to enjoy themselves once more, Brer Rabbit hollered out:

"When a big man like me chews tobacco, where is he going to spit?"

The other creatures called back as though they were getting pretty angry:

"Big man or little man, spit where you please!"

Then Brer Rabbit called out, "This is the way a big man spits," and with that he tipped over the bowl of dirty water, and when the other creatures heard it coming sloshing down the stairs, my, how they rushed out of the house! Some went out the back door, some went out the front door, some fell out of the windows, some went one way and some another way; but they all got out as quickly as they could.

Then Brer Rabbit, he shut up the house, and fastened the windows and went to bed. He pulled the covers up round his ears, and he slept like a man who doesn't owe anybody anything.

"And neither did he owe them," said Uncle Remus to the little boy, "for if the other creatures got scared and ran off from their own house, what business is that of Brer Rabbit? That's what I'd like to know."

RIDE A COCK-HORSE

Ride a cock-horse to Banbury Cross,
To see a fine lady upon a white horse;
Rings on her fingers and bells on her toes,
She shall have music wherever she goes.

BOBBY SHAFTOE

Bobby Shaftoe's gone to sea,
Silver buckles on his knee;
He'll come back and marry me,
    Bonny Bobby Shaftoe.

Bobby Shaftoe's bright and fair,
Combing down his yellow hair,
He's my love for evermore,
    Bonny Bobby Shaftoe.

Country Mouse, Town Mouse

There was once a little mouse who lived very happily in the country. He ate grains of wheat and grass seeds, nibbled turnips in the fields, and had a safe snug house in a hedgerow. On sunny days he would curl up on the bank near his nest and warm himself, and in the winter he would scamper in the fields with his friends.

He was delighted when he heard his cousin from the town was coming to visit him, and fetched some of the best food from his store cupboard so he could share it with him. When his cousin arrived, he proudly offered him some fine grains of dried wheat and some particularly good nuts he had put away in the autumn.

His cousin, the town mouse, however, was not impressed. "You call this good food?" he asked. "My dear fellow, you must come and stay with me in the city. I will then show you what fine living is all about. Come with me tomorrow, for not a day should be lost before you see the excellent hospitality I can offer."

So the two mice travelled up to town. From his cousin's mousehole, the country mouse watched with wonder a grand dinner which the people who lived in the house were giving. He stared in amazement at the variety of cheese, the beautiful vegetables, the fresh white rolls, the fruit, and the wine served from glittering decanters.

"Now's our chance," said the town mouse, as the dining-room emptied. The two mice came out of the hole, and scurried across the floor to where the crumbs lay scattered beneath the table. Never had the country mouse eaten such delicacies, or tasted such fine food. "My cousin was right," he thought as he nibbled at a fine juicy grape. "This is the good life!"

All of a sudden a great fierce furry beast leapt into the room and pounced on the mice.

"Run for it, little cousin!" shouted the town mouse, and together they reached the mousehole gasping for breath and shaking with fright. The cat settled down outside the hole, tail twitching, to wait for them.

"Don't worry. He will get bored soon, and go and amuse himself elsewhere. We can then go and finish our feast," said the town mouse.

"You can go out there again, if you like," said the country mouse. "I shall not. I am leaving tonight by the back door to return to my country home. I would rather gnaw a humble vegetable there than live here amidst these dangers."

So the country mouse lived happily in the country, the town mouse in the town. Each was content with the way of life he was used to, and had no desire to change.

HANNAH BANTRY

Hannah Bantry,
In the pantry,
Gnawing at a mutton bone;
How she gnawed it,
How she clawed it,
When she found herself alone.

A NAIL

For want of a nail
    the shoe was lost,
For want of a shoe
    the horse was lost,
For want of a horse
    the rider was lost,
For want of a rider
    the battle was lost,
For want of a battle
    the kingdom was lost,
And all for the want
    of a horseshoe nail.

LITTLE TOMMY TITTLEMOUSE

Little Tommy Tittlemouse
Lived in a little house;
He caught fishes
In other men's ditches.

BABY BUNTING

Bye, baby bunting,
Daddy's gone a-hunting,
Gone to get a rabbit skin
To wrap the baby bunting in.

The Selfish Giant

Every afternoon, as they were coming from school, the children used to go and play in the Giant's garden.

It was a large lovely garden, with soft green grass. Here and there over the grass stood beautiful flowers like stars, and there were twelve peach-trees that in the spring-time broke out into delicate blossoms of pink and pearl, and in the autumn bore rich fruit. The birds sat on the trees and sang so sweetly that the children used to stop their games in order to listen to them. "How happy we are here!" they cried to each other.

One day the Giant came back. He had been to visit his friend the Cornish ogre, and had stayed with him for seven years. After the seven years were over he had said all that he had to say, for his conversation was limited, and he was determined to return to his own castle. When he arrived he saw the children playing in the garden.

"What are you doing here?" he cried in a very gruff voice, and the children ran away.

"My own garden is my own garden," said the Giant; "any-one can understand that, and I will allow nobody to play in it but myself." So he built a high wall all round it, and put up a notice-board.

TRESPASSERS WILL BE PROSECUTED

He was a very selfish giant.

The poor children had nowhere to play. They tried to play in the road, but the road was very dusty and full of hard stones, and they did not like it. They used to wander around the high walls when their lessons were over, and talk about the beautiful garden inside. "How happy we were there!" they said to each other.

Then the Spring came, and all over the country there were little blossoms and little birds. Only in the garden of the Selfish Giant it was still winter. The birds did not care to sing in it as there were no children, and the trees forgot to blossom. Once a beautiful flower put its head out from the grass, but when it saw the notice-board it was so sorry for the children that it slipped back into the ground again and went off to sleep. The only people who were pleased were the Snow and the Frost.

"Spring has forgotten this garden," they cried, "so we will live here all the year round."

The Snow covered up the grass with her great white cloak, and the Frost painted all the trees silver. Then they invited the North Wind to stay with them, and he came. He was wrapped in furs, and he roared all day about the garden, and blew the

chimney-pots down. "This is a delightful spot," he said. "We must ask the Hail on a visit." So the Hail came. Every day for three hours he rattled on the roof of the castle till he broke most of the slates, and then ran round and round the garden as fast as he could. He was dressed in grey, and his breath was like ice.

"I cannot understand why the Spring is so late in coming," said the Selfish Giant, as he sat at the window and looked out at his cold, white garden; "I hope there will be a change in the weather."

But the Spring never came, nor the Summer. The Autumn gave golden fruit to every garden, but to the Giant's garden she gave none. "He is too selfish," she said. So it was always winter there, and the North Wind and the Hail, and the Frost, and the Snow danced about through the trees.

One morning the Giant was lying awake in bed when he heard some lovely music. It sounded so sweet to his ears that he thought it must be the King's musicians passing by. It was really only a little linnet singing outside his window, but it was so long since he had heard a bird sing in his garden that it seemed to him to be the most beautiful music in the world. Then the Hail stopped dancing over his head, and the North Wind stopped roaring, and a delicious perfume came to him through the open casement. "I believe the Spring has come at last," said the Giant; and he jumped out of bed and looked out.

What did he see?

He saw a most wonderful sight. Through a little hole in the wall the children had crept in, and they were sitting in the branches of the trees. In every tree that he could see there was a little child. And the trees were so glad to have the children back again that they had covered themselves with blossom, and were waving their arms gently above the children's heads. The birds were flying about and twittering with delight, and the flowers were looking up through the green grass and laughing.

It was a lovely scene, only in one corner was it still winter. It was the farthest corner of the garden, and in it was standing a little boy. He was so small that he could not reach up to the branches of the tree, and he was wandering all round it, crying bitterly. The poor tree was still covered with frost and snow, and the North Wind was blowing and roaring above it. "Climb up! little boy," said the Tree, and it bent its branches down as low as it could: but the boy was too tiny.

And the Giant's heart melted as he looked out. "How selfish I have been!" he said; "now I know why the Spring would not come here. I will put that little boy on the top of the tree, and then I will knock down the wall, and my garden shall be the children's playground for ever and ever." He was really very sorry for what he had done.

So he crept downstairs and opened the front door quite softly, and went out into the garden. But when the children saw him they were so frightened that they all ran away, and the garden became winter again. Only the little boy did not run, for his eyes were so full of tears that he did not see the Giant coming. And the Giant stole up behind him and took him gently in his hand, and put him up into the tree. And the tree broke at once into blossom, and the birds came and sang on it, and the little boy stretched out his two arms and flung them around the Giant's neck, and kissed him. And the other children when they saw that the Giant was not wicked any longer, came running back, and with them came the Spring. "It is your garden now, little children," said the Giant, and he took a great axe and knocked down the wall. And when the people were going to market at twelve o'clock they found the giant playing with the children in the most beautiful garden they had ever seen.

All day long they played, and in the evening the children came to the Giant to bid him good-bye.

"But where is your little companion?" he said, "the boy I put into the tree." The Giant loved him best because he had kissed him.

"We don't know," answered the children: "he has gone away."

"You must tell him to be sure and come tomorrow," said the Giant. But the children said that they did not know where he lived, and had never seen him before; and the Giant felt very sad.

Every afternoon, when school was over, the children played with the Giant. But the little boy whom the Giant loved was never seen again. The Giant was very kind to all the children, yet he longed for his first little friend, and often spoke of him. "How I would like to see him!" he used to say.

Years went over, and the Giant grew very old and feeble. He could not play about any more, so he sat in a huge armchair, and watched the children at their games, and admired his garden. "I have many beautiful flowers," he said; "but the children are the most beautiful flowers of all."

One winter morning he looked out of his window as he was dressing. He did not hate the Winter now, for he knew it was merely the Spring asleep, and that the flowers were resting.

Suddenly he rubbed his eyes in wonder and looked and looked. It certainly was a marvellous sight. In the farthest corner of the garden was a tree quite covered with lovely white blossoms. Its branches were golden, and silver fruit hung down from them, and underneath it stood the little boy he had loved.

Downstairs ran the Giant in great joy, and out into the garden. He hastened across the grass, and came near to the child. And

when he came quite close his face grew red with anger, and he said, "Who hath dared to wound thee?" For on the palms of the child's hands were the prints of two nails, and the prints of two nails were on the little feet.

"Who hath dared to wound thee?" cried the Giant; "tell me that I may take my big sword and slay him."

"Nay," answered the child: "but these are the wounds of Love."

"Who art thou?" said the Giant, and a strange awe fell on him and he knelt before the little child.

And the child smiled on the Giant, and said to him, "You let me play once in your garden, today you shall come with me to my garden, which is Paradise."

And when the children ran in that afternoon, they found the Giant lying dead under the tree, all covered with white blossoms.

LITTLE MISS MUFFET

Little Miss Muffet
Sat on a tuffet,
Eating her curds and whey;
Along came a spider,
And sat down beside her
And frightened Miss Muffet away.

THREE MEN IN A TUB

Rub-a-dub-dub,
Three men in a tub,
And how do you think they got there?
The butcher, the baker,
The candlestick-maker,
They all jumped out of a rotten potato,
'Twas enough to make a man stare.

The Three Wishes

One day a poor woodcutter was working in the forest chopping down trees and sawing them into logs. He stopped for a moment and saw a fairy sitting on a leaf nearby.

"I have come," she told him, "to give you three wishes. The next three wishes you make will come true. Use them wisely."

After work, the woodcutter returned home and told his wife what had happened. She did not believe a word he said.

"You've just dreamt it," she laughed. "Still, just in case, you'd better think carefully before you wish."

Together they wondered. Should they wish for gold, jewels, a fine home? They argued and disagreed about everything until the woodcutter shouted crossly,

"I'm hungry after all my work. Let's eat first."

"I'm afraid there's only soup," his wife replied. "I'd no money to buy any meat."

"Soup again!" grumbled the woodcutter. "How I wish that we had a fine fat sausage to eat tonight."

Before they could blink, a fine fat sausage appeared on their kitchen table.

"You idiot!" screeched his wife. "Now you've wasted one of our precious wishes. You make me so angry." She went on scolding until he could stand it no more and he shouted,

"I wish that sausage was on the end of your nose!"

Immediately the large sausage jumped in the air and attached itself to the wife's nose. There she stood with the big fat sausage hanging down in front of her. It was difficult to talk with it hanging there and she became really angry when the woodcutter laughed at her because she looked so ridiculous. She pulled and pulled; he pulled and pulled. But the sausage stayed there, stuck on the end of her nose.

The woodcutter soon stopped laughing when he remembered they only had one of the fairy's wishes left.

"Let's wish," he said quickly, "for all the riches in the world."

"What good would that do," she asked, "with a long sausage hanging from my nose? I could not enjoy them for a minute!"

The woodcutter and his wife finally agreed that they could do nothing except get rid of that sausage-nose.

The woodcutter wished and in a flash the sausage was gone, and he and his wife sat down to eat the soup that she had prepared for their supper. The only point they could agree on for a long while was how foolish they had both been to use the fairy's wishes so unwisely. They also wished – too late by now – that they had eaten the sausage when it had first appeared.

POLLY

Polly, put the kettle on,
Polly, put the kettle on,
Polly, put the kettle on,
   We'll all have tea.

Sukey, take it off again,
Sukey, take it off again,
Sukey, take it off again,
   They've all gone away.

TEN O'CLOCK SCHOLAR

A dillar, a dollar,
A ten o'clock scholar,
What makes you come so soon?
You used to come at ten o'clock,
But now you come at noon.

ONE MISTY, MOISTY MORNING

One misty, moisty morning,
    When cloudy was the weather,
There I met an old man
    Clothed all in leather.

He began to compliment,
    And I began to grin,
How do you do, and how do you do,
    And how do you do again?

SEE-SAW, MARGERY DAW

See-saw, Margery Daw,
Jacky shall have a new master;
He shall have but a penny a day,
Because he can't work any faster.

SIX LITTLE MICE

Six little mice sat down to spin;
Pussy passed by and she peeped in.
What are you doing, my little men?
Weaving coats for gentlemen.
Shall I come in and cut off your threads?
No, no, Mistress Pussy, you'd bite off our heads.
Oh, no, I'll not; I'll help you to spin.
That may be so, but you don't come in.

TO THE MAGPIE

Magpie, magpie, flutter and flee,
Turn up your tail and good luck come to me.
One for sorrow, two for joy,
Three for a girl, four for a boy,
Five for silver, six for gold,
Seven for a secret ne'er to be told.

The Little House

Once upon a time a large earthenware jar rolled off the back of a cart that was going to market. It came to rest in the grass at the side of the road.

By and by a mouse came along and looked at the jar. "What a fine house that would make," he thought, and he called out:

"Little house, little house,
Who lives in the little house?"

Nobody answered so the mouse peeped in and saw that it was empty. He moved in straightaway and began to live there.

Before long a frog came along and saw the jar. "What a fine house that would make," he thought, and he called out:

"Little house, little house,
Who lives in the little house?"

and he heard:

"I, Mr Mouse.
I live in the little house.
Who are you?"

"I am Mr Frog," came the reply.

"Come in Mr Frog, and we can live here together," called out the mouse.

So the mouse and the frog lived happily together in the little house. Then one day a hare came running along the road and saw the little house. He called out:

"Little house, little house,
Who lives in the little house?"

and he heard:

"Mr Frog and Mr Mouse,
We live in the little house.
Who are you?"
"I am Mr Hare," he replied.
"Come in Mr Hare and live with us," called the mouse and the frog.

The hare went in and settled down with the frog and the mouse in the little house.

Some time later a fox came along, and spied the little house. "That would make a fine house," he thought, and he called out:
"Little house, little house,
Who lives in the little house?"
and he heard:
"Mr Hare, Mr Frog and Mr Mouse,
We all live in the little house.
Who are you?"
"I am Mr Fox," he replied.
"Then come in and live with us, Mr Fox," they called back.

Mr Fox went in and found there was just room for him too, although it was a bit of a squeeze.

The next day a bear came ambling along the road, and saw the little house. He called out:
"Little house, little house,
Who lives in the little house?"
and he heard:
"Mr Fox, Mr Hare, Mr Frog and Mr Mouse,
We all live in the little house.
Who are you?"
"I am Mr Bear Squash-you-all-flat," said the bear.

He then sat down on the little house, and squashed it all flat.
That was the end of the little house.

I SAW A SHIP A-SAILING

I saw a ship a-sailing,
    A-sailing on the sea,
And, oh, but it was laden
    With pretty things for thee!

There were comfits in the cabin,
    And apples in the hold;
The sails were made of silk,
    And the masts were made of gold.

The four-and-twenty sailors,
    That stood between the decks,
Were four-and-twenty white mice
    With chains about their necks.

The captain was a duck
    With a packet on his back,
And when the ship began to move
    The captain said, Quack! Quack!

THE MILKMAID

Little maid, pretty maid,
  Whither goest thou?
Down to the meadow
  To milk my cow.
Shall I go with thee?
  No, not now.
When I send for thee,
  Then come thou.

The Fisherman's Son

A long time ago, when impossible things were possible, there was a fisherman and his son. One day when the fisherman hauled in his net he found a huge gleaming red fish amongst the rest of his catch. For a few moments he was so excited he could only stare at it. "This fish will make me famous," he thought. "Never before has a fisherman caught such a fish."

"Stay here," he said to his son, "and look after these fish, while I go and fetch the cart to take them home."

The fisherman's son, too, was amazed by the great red fish, and while he was waiting for his father, he stroked it and started to talk to it.

"It seems a shame that a beautiful creature like you should not swim free," he said, and no sooner had he spoken than he decided to put the fish back into the sea. The great red fish slipped gratefully into the water, raised its head and spoke to the boy.

"It was kind of you to save my life. Take this bone which I have pulled from my fin. If ever you need my help, hold it up, call me, and I will come at once."

The fisherman's son placed the bone carefully in his pocket just as his father reappeared with the cart. When the father saw that the great red fish was gone he was angry beyond belief.

"Get out of my sight," he shouted at his son, "and never let me set eyes on you again."

The boy went off sadly. He did not know where to go or what to do. In time he found himself in a great forest. He walked on and on, till suddenly he was startled by a stag rushing through the trees towards him. It was being chased by a pack of ferocious hounds followed by hunters, and it was clearly exhausted and could run no further. The boy felt sorry for the stag and took hold of its antlers as the hounds and then the hunters appeared.

"Shame on you," he said, "for chasing a tame stag. Go and find a wild beast to hunt for your sport."

The hunters, seeing the stag standing quietly by the boy, thought it must be a pet and so they turned and rode off to another part of the forest.

"It was kind of you to save my life," said the stag, and it pulled a fine brown hair from its coat. "Take this and if ever you need help, hold it out and call me. I will come at once."

The fisherman's son put the hair in his pocket with the fishbone. He thanked the stag which disappeared among the trees and wandered on once more.

As he walked he heard a strange fluttering sound overhead and, looking up, he saw a great bird – a crane – being attacked by an eagle. The crane was weak and could fight no more, and the eagle was about to kill it. The kind-hearted boy picked up a stick and threw it at the eagle, which flew off at once, fearful of this new enemy. The crane sank to the ground.

"It was kind of you to save my life," it said as it recovered its breath. "Take this feather and keep it safe. If ever you need help, hold it out and call me, and I will come."

As the fisherman's son walked on with the feather in his pocket, he met a fox running for its life, with the hounds and the huntsmen close behind. The boy just had time to hide the fox under his coat before the hounds were all around him.

"I think the fox went that way," he cried to the huntsmen, and they called off the hounds and went in the direction the boy was pointing.

"It was kind of you to save my life," said the fox. "Take this hair from my coat and keep it safe. If ever you need help, hold it out and call me. I will come at once."

The fisherman's son went on his way, and in time he reached the edge of the forest and found himself by a lovely castle.

"Who lives there?" he asked.

"A beautiful princess," he was told. "Are you one of her suitors? She plays a curious game of hide-and-seek with all who come, and says she will marry the first man who hides so well that she cannot find him."

The fisherman's son thought he would try, so boldly he went to the castle and asked to see the princess. She was indeed very beautiful, and he thought what a fine thing it would be if he could marry her.

"Princess, I will hide where you cannot find me," he said, "but will you give me four chances?"

The princess was intrigued by this shabby boy, and agreed, thinking she would at least have some fun looking for him.

The fisherman's son went straightaway to the place where he had last seen the fish and, taking the fishbone from his pocket, he called its name.

"I am here," said the great red fish. "What can I do for you?"

"Can you take me where the princess will never find me? If you do, I shall be able to marry her."

The red fish took the boy on its back and swam deep down into the sea to some caverns where it hid him.

Now the princess had a magic mirror which she used in her games of hide-and-seek. With it she could see far and wide even through houses and hillsides. She looked in her mirror, but could not find the fisherman's son.

"What a wizard he must be," she said to herself, as she turned her mirror this way and that. Then she saw him sitting in a rocky cavern deep down in the sea and she laughed.

The next day when the boy came to the palace she smiled and said, "That was easy. You were deep down in a cavern under the sea. You will have to do better than that if you are going to marry me!"

"What an enchantress she must be," said the boy to himself, and he resolved to win this contest.

He went next to the forest and held out the stag's hair and called. When the stag came he told it that he wanted to hide and the stag took him on its back far far away to the other side of the mountains and hid him in a little cave. The stag then stood in front of the cave so that no one could see inside.

Once more the princess took out her mirror and searched far and wide for the boy. "How clever he is," she said to herself, and then the mirror picked him out hiding in the cave.

The next day she said to the boy, "Pooh! It was easy to see you in that cave."

The boy became even more determined to marry her and he set out to summon the crane. It came as soon as the boy waved the feather and called its name.

"Come with me high up into the clouds," said the crane, and took the boy on its back. All day long they hovered in the sky, while the princess searched this way and that in her mirror.

Just as she was about to give up, she spied him above her. "He is cleverer than I thought!" she said to herself.

But the next day when the boy came to the castle, she laughed and said, "You thought I would never find you among the clouds, but I spotted you easily. You only have one more chance to outwit me!"

The boy now went to the forest and, holding up the fox's hair he called the fox. When it came he explained what he wanted. "Ask her to give you fourteen days," said the fox, "and I should be able to hide you where she cannot find you."

The princess agreed, and for fourteen days the fox tunnelled and dug beneath the princess's castle until it had made a hole large enough for the boy to hide in right under the princess's room. Down he went and lay there quietly. The princess took out her mirror and searched. She looked to the north, to the south, to the east, to the west; she looked high and low, round and round, and at last, exasperated, she called out:

"I give up. Where are you, fisherman's son?"

"Here!" he called. "Just below you!" And he jumped out from the hole the fox had dug.

"You win, wizard," she said, and was happy to marry the fisherman's son.

He was delighted to marry such a beautiful princess. They had a great wedding in the castle, and the celebrations went on for many days.

SING A SONG OF SIXPENCE

Sing a song of sixpence,
  A pocket full of rye;
Four-and-twenty blackbirds,
  Baked in a pie.

When the pie was opened,
  The birds began to sing;
Was not that a dainty dish,
  To set before the king?

The king was in his counting-house,
  Counting out his money;
The queen was in the parlour
  Eating bread and honey.

The maid was in the garden,
  Hanging out the clothes,
When down came a blackbird
  And pecked off her nose.

The Little Red Hen and the Fox

A little red hen lived all alone in a house in the forest. She was a houseproud little hen who always kept her house neat and tidy. She always wore an apron and in the pocket she kept scissors and a needle and thread, for she always said, "You never know when they will come in handy."

Now the little red hen had one enemy – a rascally fox who lived over the hill. The fox used to lie awake at night thinking how much he would enjoy eating the little red hen. But the little red hen took great care not to fall into any of the fox's traps when she was out in the forest, and in the evening she always stayed at home. What is more, she always locked her door when she went out and slipped the key into her pocket with the scissors and needle and thread, so that the greedy fox could not creep into her house and surprise her when she came home. She locked the door behind her too, whenever she was inside the house.

The fox used to watch her from behind a tree, and one day he said to his old mother who lived with him, "Mother! Stoke up the fire, and keep a big pot boiling, for tonight I am going to catch the little red hen. I have worked out a plan which will not fail."

The fox took a sack, slung it over his shoulder, and set out over the hill to catch the little red hen. He crept as close as he could to the little red hen's house, and there he lay in wait.

Sure enough, before he had been there an hour, the little red hen came out.

She was just going to the wood pile to bring in some wood, so she did not bother to lock the door behind her. Quick as a flash that old rascal the fox was inside her house with his sack, and was waiting for her as she returned with some sticks.

"Hello there, little red hen," he called out as she shut the door. "I have caught you now, and you are coming home with me for my supper!"

With a flurry of feathers and a great deal of squawking, the little red hen flew out of the fox's reach, and settled on the rafters above his head.

"Don't you be so sure of yourself, you old rascal," said the little red hen. "You can't reach me up here."

That was true. The fox sat down wondering what to do next, and all the while the little red hen sat up in the rafters hoping the fox would get bored or hungry and go and look for his supper elsewhere. But foxes are not called cunning for nothing, and the

old rascal soon had a plan. He started to twirl and turn, round and round, chasing his own tail. Faster and faster he went until the whole house seemed to be full of twirling red fox.

The little red hen grew so dizzy watching him spin that she lost her balance and fell off her rafter with a great thud. In a trice the fox bundled her into his sack, flung it over his shoulder and set out over the hill to his home.

At first, the little red hen was confused by her dizziness and the fall, and by the darkness in the sack, but her mind soon cleared, and she lay quietly waiting for a chance to escape.

The fox, even though he had succeeded in bringing the little red hen down off the rafters, was still feeling quite dizzy and breathless from all that spinning around. So on the way home he sat down for a rest and put the sack on the ground beside him. In no time at all, the little red hen had taken her scissors from her pocket and snip, snip, snip, she cut her way out of the sack. She saw a stone nearby and rolled it into the sack and, while the fox was lying back chuckling to himself, that little red hen stitched up the hole. She finished sewing and just had time to hide behind a tree before the fox took up the sack once more and hurried on over the hill to his own house.

"Here I am, mother," he called, as he came into his house. "Is the pot boiling? The little red hen is in the sack."

"Everything is ready," replied his mother. "Put the hen straight into the boiling water."

"Here she comes," said the fox, as he opened the sack and emptied it into the cooking pot.

Splash! The stone fell into the water.

"That's a very odd hen," shrieked the fox's mother. "How dare you fool me like that!" But the fox knew that it was he who had been fooled by the little red hen.

He and his mother went to bed hungry that night, and the next day the fox went hunting for his supper elsewhere. As for the little red hen, she went home and, for the rest of her days, she always carried a pair of scissors and a needle and thread in her pocket, and she would always say with a smile, "You never know when they will come in handy."

THE CROOKED MAN

There was a crooked man,
    And he walked a crooked mile,
He found a crooked sixpence
    Against a crooked stile;
He bought a crooked cat,
    Which caught a crooked mouse,
And they all lived together
    In a little crooked house.

JACK

Jack, be nimble,
    Jack, be quick,
Jack, jump over
    The candlestick.

THE MULBERRY BUSH

Here we go round the mulberry bush,
The mulberry bush, the mulberry bush,
Here we go round the mulberry bush,
On a cold and frosty morning.

PEASE PORRIDGE

Pease porridge hot,
Pease porridge cold,
Pease porridge in the pot,
Nine days old.
Some like it hot,
Some like it cold,
Some like it in the pot,
Nine days old.

Sleeping Beauty

Long ago there lived a king and queen who had no children, which made them very sad. Then, one day, the queen was delighted to find she was going to have a baby. She and the king looked forward with great excitement to the day of their first child's birth.

When that day came, a lovely daughter was born and they arranged a large party for her christening. They invited many guests, including twelve fairies as they felt certain the fairies would make wishes for their little daughter.

At the christening party, the guests and the fairies all agreed that the princess was a beautiful baby. One fairy wished for her the gift of Happiness, another Beauty, others Wisdom, Health, Goodness, Contentment ... Eleven fairies had made their wishes when suddenly the gates of the castle flew open and in swept a thirteenth fairy. She was furious that she had not been invited to the christening party, and as she glared at the other fairies a shiver ran down everyone's spine. All felt her evil spirit. She waved her wand over the baby and cast not a wish but a terrible spell.

"On her sixteenth birthday," she hissed, "the princess will prick herself with a spindle. And she will die." A terrible hush fell over the king and queen and their guests.

The twelfth fairy had not yet made her wish. She had been going to give the gift of Joy to the baby but now she wanted to save the princess. Her magic was not strong enough to break the wicked spell but she could weaken its evil. So she wished that the princess, instead of dying on her sixteenth birthday, would fall asleep for a hundred years.

As she grew up the princess became the happiest, sweetest and most beautiful child anyone had ever seen. It seemed as though all the wishes of the first eleven fairies had come true. The king and queen hoped to prevent the wicked fairy's spell from working by making sure the princess never saw a spindle. All spinning was forbidden everywhere and all the cotton and wool in their country had to be sent away to be spun.

For their daughter's sixteenth birthday the king and queen decided to give a party in the castle. They felt sure there would be no chance of her finding a spindle there on the day.

People came from far and near to the grand birthday ball for the princess and a magnificent feast was provided. After the guests had eaten and drunk as much as they wanted and danced in the great hall, the princess asked if they could all play her favourite childhood game, hide-and-seek. She ran off to a far corner of the castle and found herself climbing a spiral staircase in a turret she did not remember even noticing before. "They will never find me here," she thought as she crept into a little room at the top. To her astonishment there was an old woman dressed in black and sitting on a stool, spinning.

"What are you doing?" asked the princess as she watched the twirling spindle. She was puzzled as she had never seen anything like it anywhere in the kingdom.

"Come and see," replied the old woman. She pulled strands of wool from the sheep's fleece on the floor and, twisting it neatly with her fingers, she fed it through the spindle. The princess was fascinated and edged nearer.

"Would you like to try?" asked the old woman cunningly.

The princess forgot all about playing hide-and-seek and picked up the spindle. As she did so she pricked her thumb. With a small cry she fell to the ground, as though dead. The wicked fairy's spell seemed to have worked after all.

But so did the twelfth fairy's wish. The princess did not die but fell into a deep deep sleep. The spell worked on everyone else in the castle too. The king and queen slept on their thrones in the great hall. The guests dropped off to sleep as they played hide-and-seek. And in the kitchen the cook fell asleep with her hand raised to box the pot-boy's ears. All over the castle a great silence descended.

As time went by a thorn hedge grew up around the castle. Passers-by wondered what lay behind the hedge but no one now remembered the castle where the king and queen had lived with their lovely daughter. Sometimes curious travellers tried to force their way through but the hedge was so prickly that they soon gave up.

One day, many many years later, a prince came riding past. He too marvelled at the thorn hedge which had now grown very tall and thick. An old man told him a story he had heard as a child long ago, about a mysterious castle there, and the prince became curious. He decided to cut his way through the thorns. To his surprise the hedge seemed to open out before his sword and very soon the young prince was inside the grounds. He ran across the gardens and through an open door into the lovely old castle.

Everywhere he looked – in the great hall, in the kitchen, in the ballroom and on the staircase – he saw people asleep. He hurried through many rooms until he found himself climbing a winding stair to an old turret. There in the small room at the top he was startled to discover the most beautiful girl he had ever seen. She was so lovely that without thinking he knelt down and gently kissed her.

The spell was broken. The princess opened her eyes and fell in love then and there with the prince. She told him what had happened and he kissed her again. Together they came down the turret stairs and saw that the castle was coming alive.

In the great hall the king and queen were stretching and yawning, puzzled and worried that they had dropped off to sleep during their daughter's party. Their guests too were shaking their heads, rubbing their eyes, and wondering why they felt so sleepy. In the kitchen the cook boxed the pot-boy's ear. Outside horses neighed, dogs barked and birds burst into song. The hundred-year spell had been completely broken.

The princess told her parents that she truly loved the

166

handsome young man who had kissed her. The king and queen gave the couple their blessing and a grand royal wedding was arranged.

The twelve good fairies who had come to the christening were invited once more and everyone rejoiced to see the happiness of the prince and princess. Towards evening they rode off together to their new home in the prince's kingdom, where they lived happily ever afterwards. The thirteenth fairy was never seen again.

LITTLE BOY BLUE

Little Boy Blue,
  Come blow your horn.
The sheep's in the meadow,
  The cow's in the corn.
Where is the boy
  Who looks after the sheep?
He's under a haystack
  Fast asleep.
Will you wake him?
  No, not I,
For if I do,
  He's sure to cry.

TO THE LADYBIRD

Ladybird, ladybird,
    Fly away home,
Your house is on fire
    Your children all gone;
All but one,
    And her name is Ann,
And she has crept under
    The warming pan.

GREGORY GRIGGS

Gregory Griggs, Gregory Griggs,
Had twenty-seven different wigs.
He wore them up, he wore them down,
To please the people of the town;
He wore them east, he wore them west,
But he never could tell which he loved the best.

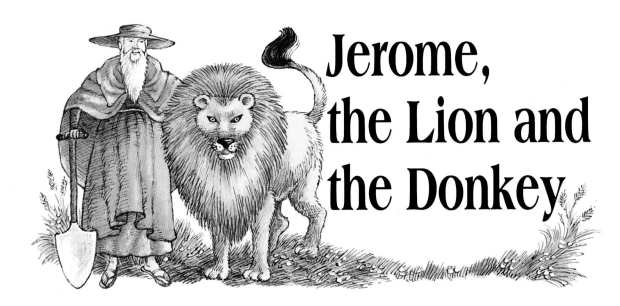

Jerome, the Lion and the Donkey

Jerome was a holy man who lived in a monastery many hundreds of years ago. One hot afternoon, he and some of the other monks were sitting together, when a lion appeared in the courtyard of the monastery. There was panic and confusion as several of the monks thought the lion had come to kill them, but then Jerome saw that the lion was limping.

"Calm yourselves, brothers," he said, "and bring me some clean cloths and warm water. The poor creature has come to us for help. We need not be afraid of him."

Cautiously they gathered round, and one man fetched warm water, another a clean cloth for a bandage, and another some ointment made from healing herbs. Very gently, Jerome bathed and bandaged the torn foot. The lion then lay down peacefully in the shade of the courtyard and slept.

The next day the lion was still there, and Jerome bathed his paw again. It was less swollen, and again the lion seemed grateful for the help he had received. So it was for several days, until the paw was completely healed. The monks were pleased to hear he was cured, as they thought he would now go away.

But the lion did not go. He stayed and followed Jerome when he went to work in the fields, and lay down in the courtyard when Jerome was in the monastery. Several monks felt certain that a fully grown lion, no longer in pain, must be savage, and that sooner or later someone would be hurt. But whenever they tried sending the lion away he always came back to the monastery.

"It's no good," said Jerome. "He has come to stay."

170

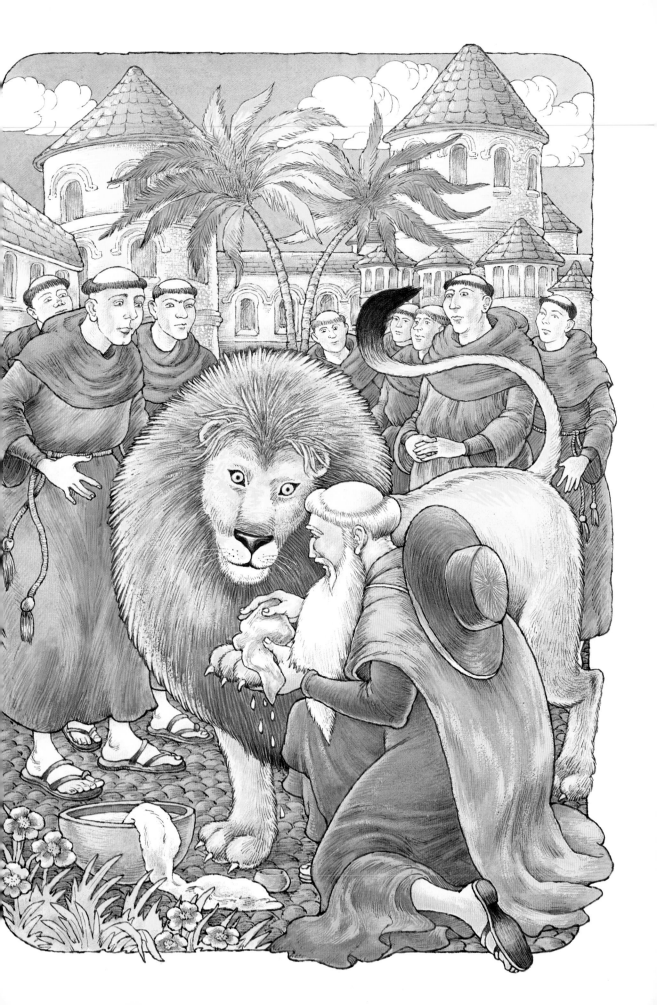

"It is not right that he should stay for he does no work," said one of the monks. "None of us stays here without working."

So Jerome said, "Well, let us think of some work he can do."

Then one old monk whose job it was to take the donkey to the woods every day to collect logs for the fire, said, "Let the lion go with the donkey each day. He will stop wild beasts attacking the donkey better than I can, and I will then be free to do other jobs."

So it was agreed, and each day the lion and the donkey set out together for the woods. On the way the donkey would eat grass in the pasture while the lion guarded him. The woodmen would then fill the baskets that were strapped to the donkey's back with logs, and together they would return.

"What a useful member of the community he is," said some of the monks, while others still took care not to get too close.

One day, as the donkey was grazing, the lion found a shady spot to lie and wait for his friend, and in the still of the hot day he dropped off to sleep. As he slept some travelling merchants with a string of camels came by, and saw the donkey grazing alone.

"Look at that," they said to each other. "A donkey is just what we want to lead our camels. No one seems to be looking after it. Let's take it quickly."

The merchants threw the donkey's baskets behind a bush, and led him off at the head of their camels.

When the lion awoke and found the donkey had disappeared, he roared in misery. That evening he returned to the monastery, his head hanging low with shame. The monks crowded round him, wondering where the donkey was.

"A wild beast should never be trusted," some of them said. "He has killed and eaten our dear donkey, even after all these months of appearing to be such a gentle animal."

Jerome said, "Do not judge him too quickly, brothers. Let us go to the wood and see if we find something to show us what happened to the donkey."

So a group of monks set off, and when they found the donkey's baskets, they said, "Look, here is the evidence we wanted. This shows the donkey was killed by the savage lion."

But the lion still showed no sign of being fierce, so Jerome

suggested to the angry monks that the lion should now do the donkey's work. "Let him go to the woods each day with the donkey's baskets strapped to his back," he said, "and let him carry the logs we need as the little donkey used to do."

The monks agreed to Jerome's plan, and each morning after that the lion set out for the woods alone to collect the logs.

A whole year went by, and during this time Jerome was made the head monk in the monastery. The lion, still Jerome's friend and companion, continued to go each day to get wood for the monastery. He did the task without complaining, almost as if he were saying, "I am sorry about the donkey," each time they strapped the baskets on him.

One day, when he was returning from the woods, the lion caught sight of his old friend the donkey. The travelling merchants were once more on their old route and the little donkey they had stolen was leading their string of camels. Without hesitating, the lion gave a great roar and bounded over to the donkey. The merchants, thinking they were being attacked by a wild and ferocious lion, fled in terror, while the donkey gave a bray of delight and trotted over to his friend the lion.

Together they set off towards the monastery, for the lion wished to show the monks that he had found the little donkey. For a whole year the camels had followed the donkey, and now they

continued to do so. The merchants were all hiding and could do nothing to stop them.

At the monastery, the monks looked up in astonishment to see the strange procession of lion, donkey and camels.

"I see," said Jerome, "that the lion has made good his fault. He has found the donkey he so carelessly lost a year ago. We have been harsh to think he might have killed him."

Just then the courtyard was filled with angry merchants who had followed the camels. Now they asked to speak to the head of the monastery, and Jerome stepped forward.

"You have stolen our donkey, our camels and all our wares," they shouted angrily. "We demand you return them at once."

"We have stolen nothing," Jerome replied quietly. "Your camels and the goods they carry are yours to take away. The camels came here of their own accord. But the donkey is not yours

to take. He was ours, and he was stolen last year. It must have been you who took him, and hid his baskets behind the bush. Now he has come back with his friend the lion to his real owners."

The merchants now looked ashamed. Promising they would not steal again and still eyeing the lion with fear, they went on their way, taking their camels and goods with them.

The donkey and the lion went out together each day as before, and the monks who had thought the lion a savage beast were sorry that they had misjudged him. The lion lived for many more years in the monastery, and in his old age he would sit at Jerome's feet as the holy man wrote books. The monastery was known far and wide as a place where wisdom and gentleness were always to be found.

TOM, TOM

Tom, Tom, the piper's son,
Stole a pig and away he run;
  The pig was eat,
    And Tom was beat,
And Tom went howling
  down the street.

OLD WOMAN

There was an old woman
  Lived under a hill,
And if she's not gone
  She lives there still.

THE OWL

A wise old owl sat in an oak,
The more he heard the less he spoke;
The less he spoke the more he heard.
Why aren't we all like that wise old bird?

LUCY LOCKET

Lucy Locket lost her pocket,
    Kitty Fisher found it;
Not a penny was there in it,
    But a ribbon round it.

Beauty and the Beast

Arich merchant who had three sons and three daughters lived in a big house in the city. His youngest daughter was so beautiful she was called Beauty by all who knew her. She was as sweet and good as she was beautiful. Sadly all of the merchant's ships were lost at sea and he and his family had to move to a small cottage in the country. His sons worked hard on the land and Beauty was happy working in the house, but his two elder daughters complained and grumbled all day long, especially about Beauty.

One day news came that a ship had arrived which would make the merchant wealthy again. The merchant set off to the city, and just before he left he said, "Tell me, daughters, what gifts would you like me to bring back for you?"

The two older girls asked for fine clothes and jewels, but Beauty wanted nothing. Realizing this made her sisters look greedy, she thought it best to ask for something. "Bring me a rose, father," she said, "just a beautiful red rose."

When the merchant reached the city he found disaster had struck once more and the ship's cargo was ruined. He took the road home wondering how to break the news to his children. He was so deep in thought that he lost his way. Worse still, it started to snow, and he feared he would never reach home alive. Just as he despaired he noticed lights ahead, and riding towards them he saw a fine castle. The gates stood open and flares were alight in the courtyard. In the stables a stall stood empty with hay in the manger and clean bedding on the floor ready for his horse.

The castle itself seemed to be deserted, but a fire was burning in the dining-hall where a table was laid with food. The merchant ate well, and still finding no one went upstairs to a bedroom which had been prepared. "It is almost as if I were expected," he thought.

In the morning he found clean clothes had been laid out for him and breakfast was on the table in the dining-hall. After he had eaten he fetched his horse and as he rode away he saw a spray of red roses growing from a rose bush. Remembering Beauty's request, and thinking he would be able to bring a present for at least one daughter, he plucked a rose from the bush.

Suddenly a beast-like monster appeared. "Is this how you repay my hospitality?" it roared. "You eat my food, sleep in my guest-room and then insult me by stealing my flowers. You shall die for this."

The merchant pleaded for his life, and begged to see his children once more before he died. At last the beast relented.

"I will spare your life," it said, "if one of your daughters will come here willingly and die for you. Otherwise you must promise to return within three months and die yourself."

The merchant agreed to return and went on his way. At home his children listened with sorrow to his tales of the lost cargo and his promise to the monster. His two elder daughters turned on Beauty, saying, "Your stupid request for a rose has brought all this trouble on us. It is your fault that father must die."

179

When the three months were up Beauty insisted on going to the castle with her father, pretending only to ride with him for company on the journey. The beast met them, and asked Beauty if she had come of her own accord, and she told him she had.

"Good," he said. "Now your father can go home and you will stay with me."

"What shall I call you?" she asked bravely.

"You may call me Beast," he replied.

Certainly he was very ugly and it seemed a good name for him. Beauty waved a sad farewell to her father. But she was happy that at least she had saved his life.

As Beauty wandered through the castle she found many lovely rooms and beautiful courtyards with gardens. At last she came to a room which was surely meant just for her. It had many of her favourite books and objects in it. On the wall hung a beautiful mirror and to her surprise, as she looked into it, she saw her father arriving back at their home and her brothers and sisters greeting him. The picture only lasted a few seconds then faded. "This Beast may be ugly, but he is certainly kind," she thought. "He gives me all the things I like and allows me to know how my family is without me."

That night at supper the Beast joined her. He sat and stared at her. At the end of the meal he asked: "Will you marry me?".

Beauty was startled by the question but said as gently as she could, "No, Beast, you are kind but I cannot marry you."

Each day it was the same. Beauty had everything she wanted during the day and each evening the Beast asked her to marry him, and she always said no.

One night Beauty dreamt that her father lay sick. She asked the Beast if she could go to him, and he refused, saying that if she left him he would die of loneliness. But when he saw how unhappy Beauty was, he said:

"If you go to your family, will you return within a week?"

"Of course," Beauty replied.

"Very well, just place this ring on your dressing table the night you wish to return, and you shall come back here. But do not stay away longer than a week, or I shall die."

The next morning Beauty awoke to find herself in her own home. Her father was indeed sick, but Beauty nursed him lovingly. Beauty's sisters were jealous once more. They thought that if she stayed at home longer than a week the Beast would kill her. So they pretended to love her and told her how much they had missed her. Before Beauty knew what had happened ten days had passed. Then she had a dream that the Beast was lying still as though he were dead by the lake near his castle.

"I must return at once," she cried and she placed her ring on the dressing table.

The next morning she found herself once more in the Beast's castle. All that day she expected to see him, but he never came. "I have killed the Beast," she cried, "I have killed him." Then she remembered that in her dream he had been by the lake and quickly she ran there. He lay still as death, down by the water's edge.

"Oh, Beast!" she wept, "Oh, Beast! I did not mean to stay away so long. Please do not die. Please come back to me. You are so good and kind." She knelt and kissed his ugly head.

Suddenly no Beast was there, but a handsome prince stood before her. "Beauty, my dear one," he said, "I was bewitched by a spell that could only be broken when a beautiful girl loved me and wanted me in spite of my ugliness. When you kissed me just now you broke the enchantment."

Beauty rode with the prince to her father's house and then they all went together to the prince's kingdom. There he and Beauty were married. In time they became king and queen, and ruled for many happy years.

GOING TO ST IVES

As I was going to St Ives,
I met a man with seven wives;
Each wife had seven sacks,
Each sack had seven cats,
Each cat had seven kits:
Kits, cats, sacks, and wives,
How many were there going to St Ives?

(One or none)

TO THE BAT

Bat, bat, come under my hat,
   And I'll give you a slice of bacon;
And when I bake, I'll give you a cake,
   If I am not mistaken.

HIGGLETY, PIGGLETY

Higglety, pigglety, pop!
The dog has eaten the mop;
   The pig's in a hurry,
   The cat's in a flurry,
Higglety, pigglety, pop!

184

THE FLYING PIG

Dickery, dickery, dare,
The pig flew up in the air;
The man in brown
Soon brought him down,
Dickery, dickery, dare.

THREE GHOSTESSES

Three little ghostesses,
Sitting on postesses,
Eating buttered toastesses,
Greasing their fistesses,
Up to their wristesses.
Oh, what beastesses
To make such feastesses!

GOOSEY GANDER

Goosey, goosey gander,
    Whither shall I wander?
Upstairs and downstairs
    And in my lady's chamber.
There I met an old man
    Who would not say his prayers,
I took him by the left leg
    And threw him down the stairs.

Three Billy Goats Gruff

Once upon a time there were three billy goats who had curly horns and tufted beards. They were known as the Three Billy Goats Gruff. They lived in a village where there was not always enough food for them, so they used to cross over a wooden bridge to the other side of the valley to munch the rich grass in the meadows there.

A deep river ran under the bridge, and beside the river and under the bridge lived a fierce troll. He had a nose as long as a poker, eyes like saucers, and teeth as sharp as knives. He hated people or animals to cross the bridge. If he could catch them, he would eat them. The three billy goats had to try and get across to the valley without disturbing the troll if they possibly could.

One day the troll was lying under the bridge when he heard the sound of steps *trip trap, trip trap* on the wooden planks above him.

"Who's that trip-trapping over my bridge?" roared the troll.

The smallest Billy Goat Gruff was on the bridge, and he called out in a small, frightened voice,

"It is only I, the little Billy Goat Gruff."

"Then I shall eat you for my dinner," roared the troll.

"No, don't," pleaded the little Billy Goat Gruff. "Let me cross over and eat the grass on the other side and I will grow fatter. My brother, the middle-sized Billy Goat Gruff, will be coming along soon. He's bigger than me. Why don't you wait and eat him?"

"Very well," grumbled the troll, and settled down under the bridge to wait for the middle-sized Billy Goat Gruff.

Before long, he heard *trip trap, trip trap* on the wooden planks above him.

"Who's that trip-trapping over my bridge?" roared the troll.

"It is I, the middle-sized Billy Goat Gruff," replied the goat in a middle-sized voice.

"Then I shall eat you for my dinner," roared the troll.

"I think," said the middle-sized Billy Goat Gruff, "you would do better to wait for my brother, the big Billy Goat Gruff. He will make a much better dinner, and meanwhile I shall be able to get fatter in those meadows over there."

"Very well," grumbled the troll and settled down to wait for the big Billy Goat Gruff.

Before long the big Billy Goat Gruff came along. The troll heard his hooves on the wooden planks above him. This time the *trip trap, trip trap* was loud and heavy.

"Who's that trip-trapping over my bridge?" roared the troll.

"It is I, the big Billy Goat Gruff," called the goat in a big gruff voice and he sounded almost as fierce as the troll.

"Then I shall eat you for my dinner," bellowed the troll.

"Oh no you won't," replied the big Billy Goat Gruff, "for I have sharp horns and will kill you first."

The troll was so angry that he leapt out from underneath the bridge. But the big Billy Goat Gruff was waiting for him with his head down and his horns ready. The troll was tossed up into the air and down into the deep river – SPLASH!

The big Billy Goat Gruff went on his way to join his two brothers, *trip trap, trip trap* over the bridge and into the meadows. Now every morning and evening the Three Billy Goats Gruff could come and go over the bridge as they pleased, and they all grew very fat indeed.

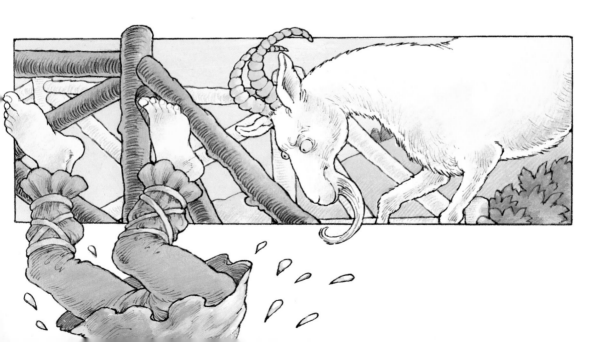

SIMPLE SIMON

Simple Simon met a pieman,
  Going to the fair;
Says Simple Simon to the pieman,
  Let me taste your ware.

Says the pieman to Simple Simon,
  Show me first your penny;
Says Simple Simon to the pieman,
  Indeed I have not any.

Simple Simon went a-fishing,
  For to catch a whale;
All the water he had got
  Was in his mother's pail.

Simple Simon went to look
  If plums grew on a thistle;
He pricked his fingers very much,
  Which made poor Simon whistle.

He went for water in a sieve
  But soon it all ran through;
And now poor Simple Simon
  Bids you all adieu.

The Black Bull of Norroway

Long ago, in a country far away in the north there lived a widow and her three daughters. She had once been a queen, but her husband, the king, had been killed in a battle and she was now very, very poor.

One day her eldest daughter said to her, "Mother, bake me a cake to take to the fortune-teller so that she will tell me my fortune."

The fortune-teller accepted the fine cake the girl had brought, and then she said to her, "Stand by the back door, my dear, and tell me if anything comes down the road."

By and by the girl cried out that a carriage drawn by six grey horses was coming towards them.

"Go with it," said the fortune-teller, "for there your fortune lies."

Before long the second daughter asked her mother to bake a cake for the fortune-teller, for she too wanted to know what life had to offer her.

"Stand by the back door, my dear," said the fortune-teller, "and tell me if anything comes down the road." When a carriage drawn by six gleaming chestnut horses came by, she told the girl to get into it, for there lay her fortune.

In time the youngest asked her mother to bake a cake for her to take to the fortune-teller. Just as before, the fortune-teller said, "Stand by the back door, my dear, and tell me if anything comes down the road." Soon the girl saw a great black bull.

"Go with the bull, girl," said the fortune-teller, "for your fortune lies with the bull."

The young girl was very disappointed, for she wanted to drive away in a fine carriage like her sisters, but she did as the fortune-teller told her.

She rode on the back of the great black bull for many miles, until she was faint with hunger and thirst. "Eat out of my left ear," said the bull, "and drink out of my right." The girl did as he suggested and to her amazement found in each ear all the food and drink she wanted.

In the evening they came to a fine castle. "We will spend the night here," said the bull, "in my brother's castle."

The girl was lifted off his back and taken into the castle while the bull was led into a field. To her surprise she found her eldest sister living there as the lady of the house. They greeted each other joyfully, then her sister said, "The black bull is really the Lord of Norroway. A spell was cast many years ago which turned him into a bull."

That night the girl slept in great luxury and the next day her sister gave her a beautiful apple. "Keep it," she said, and do not break it, until you are in great trouble."

All that day the girl travelled on the black bull's back, until evening when they came to another fine castle. "We will stay the night here, in this castle where my second brother lives," said the bull.

This time the girl found her other sister living there as a grand lady. She spent the night in a room hung with gold tapestries and in the morning her sister gave her a pear.

"Keep it safe," she said, "until the day when you are in great need. Only then should you break it open."

That day, the girl and the black bull travelled on again. Further and further they journeyed – further than the girl thought possible. She was exhausted when they arrived in the evening at a castle that was grander than any she had seen.

"This is my home," said the bull, "and we will stay here for tonight." The girl was well looked after as before and the next morning she was given a beautiful plum.

"Keep this carefully," she was told, "until the day when you are in great need. Only then should you break it open."

On the fourth day the great black bull took her to a deep dark valley, where he asked her to get off his back. "You must stay here," he said, "while I go and fight the devil. You will know if I win, for everything around will turn blue, but if I lose, everything you see will turn red. Sit on this boulder and remember you must not move, not even a hand or a foot, until I return. For if you move, I shall never find you again."

The girl promised to do as she was told, for by now she loved and trusted the bull. For hours and hours she sat on the boulder without moving, then, just when she felt she could wait no longer, everything around her suddenly went blue. She was so delighted that she moved one foot. She moved it only a little, just enough to cross it over the other, forgetting her promise for a moment.

The bull returned after his victory but, just as he had said, he could not find her anywhere. The girl stayed in the valley for hours, weeping for what she had done, and at last she set off alone, although she did not know where to go.

After she had wandered from valley to valley for several days, the young girl came to a glass mountain. She tried to climb it, but each time her feet slipped backwards, and eventually she gave up. Soon after this she met a blacksmith who told her that if she worked for him for seven years he would make her special shoes of iron that would take her over the glass mountain.

For seven long years she worked hard for the blacksmith, and at the end of that time he kept his promise and made her the shoes to take her on her way. On the other side of the mountain she stopped at a little house where a washerwoman and her daughter were scrubbing some bloodstained clothes in a tub.

"The finest lord I have ever seen left these clothes here seven years ago," said the washerwoman. "He told us that whoever washed out the bloodstains would be his wife. But for seven long years we have washed and rinsed, and the stains remain."

"Let me try," said the girl, and the first time she washed the clothes the bloodstains disappeared. Absolutely delighted, the washerwoman rushed off and told the lord of the castle nearby that the clothes were clean. Now this lord was the Lord of Norroway, and the old woman lied to him, saying that it was her own daughter who had done the task. She thought it would be a fine thing for her daughter to marry a lord. The wedding was arranged for the next day, and there seemed nothing the young girl could do to stop it.

Then she remembered the apple she had been given so long ago. Surely the time had come to open it. Inside were jewels, which sparkled and shone. She showed these to the washerwoman, and asked if she could see the lord alone that evening. "The jewels will all be yours if you arrange this for me," she said.

The washerwoman took the jewels greedily, but before she allowed the girl to go to the lord's room, she put a sleeping potion in his drink, so that he slept deeply the whole night through.

The girl sat by his bedside, and she cried:
"Seven long years I served for thee,
The glassy hill I climbed for thee,
The bloodstained clothes I washed for thee,
Wilt thou not wake, and turn to me?"
but the Lord of Norroway slept on.

The next day the girl was overcome with grief because she had failed to stop the wedding, so she broke open the pear. It contained even more lovely jewels than the apple. She took these to the washerwoman. "Marry your daughter tomorrow," she begged once again, "not today, and let me see the lord alone once more. In return the jewels will be yours."

The washerwoman agreed, but again slipped a sleeping potion into the lord's drink.

For the second time the girl sat by his bedside and cried:
"Seven long years I served for thee,
The glassy hill I climbed for thee,
The bloodstained clothes I washed for thee,
Wilt thou not wake and turn to me?"
but the Lord of Norroway slept on.

The next morning the girl broke open the beautiful plum she had been given, and found an even greater collection of splendid jewels. She offered them to the greedy washerwoman who agreed to put off the wedding one more day. That night she once more put the sleeping potion into the lord's drink. But this time the lord poured away the drink when the washerwoman was not looking for he suspected trickery of some kind.

When the girl came to his room for the third time and cried:

"Seven long years I served for thee,
The glassy hill I climbed for thee,
The bloodstained clothes I washed for thee,
Wilt thou not wake and turn to me?"

the Lord of Norroway turned and saw her.

As they talked he told her his story: how a spell had been cast on him turning him into a bull, how he had fought and beaten the devil and the spell had been broken. "Ever since then," he said, "I have been searching for you."

The Lord of Norroway and the youngest daughter were married next day, and lived happily in the castle. "I little thought," she said, "the day I saw the black bull coming down the road, that I had truly found my fortune."

BOW-WOW

Bow-wow says the dog,
Mew, mew says the cat,
Grunt, grunt goes the hog,
And squeak goes the rat.

Whoo-oo says the owl,
Caw, caw says the crow,
Quack, quack says the duck,
And what cuckoos say, you know.

ONE, TWO, THREE, FOUR, FIVE

One, two, three, four, five,
Once I caught a fish alive,
Six, seven, eight, nine, ten,
Then I let it go again.
Why did you let it go?
Because it bit my finger so.
Which finger did it bite?
This little finger on the right.

THE BELLS OF LONDON

Oranges and lemons,
Say the bells of St Clement's.

You owe me five farthings,
Say the bells of St Martin's.

When will you pay me?
Say the bells of Old Bailey.

When I grow rich,
Say the bells of Shoreditch.

When will that be?
Say the bells of Stepney.

I'm sure I don't know,
Says the Great Bell of Bow.

Here comes the candle
to light you to bed,
Here comes the chopper,
to chop off your head.

The Rats' Daughter

Mr and Mrs Rat had the most beautiful daughter. She had the longest slinkiest tail you could imagine, and the most remarkable long elegant whiskers. Her silky coat was a lovely glowing pinkish brown colour, and her teeth were gleaming white with sharp points. She was in every way a very lovely young rat.

Mr Rat was hoping to find a handsome young rat as a husband for this daughter. Mrs Rat, however, was more ambitious and hoped to marry her daughter to the most powerful creature in the world.

"I have been thinking, my dear," she said to Mr Rat one day, "that there is nothing more powerful in the world than the Sun. I feel sure the Sun would like to marry our lovely daughter."

Mr Rat was rather taken aback by this idea, but seeing that his wife's mind was made up, he agreed. So they all set off to call on the Sun.

Now the Sun was not at all interested in the idea of marrying a rat – even a very beautiful rat – but he listened politely to what the parents had to say, and thought for a few moments before replying.

"You flatter me when you say I am the most powerful thing in the world, for I am not as powerful as that Cloud you can see over there. He can stand in front of me, and shut off my light and heat whenever he wants. I think your daughter would do better to marry the Cloud."

Mr and Mrs Rat were delighted with his suggestion, for they could see at once that what the Sun had said was true. Certainly the Cloud was more powerful than the Sun, for at any time he could cover the Sun whether the Sun wanted it or not. "We should go to the Cloud with our daughter," they agreed, "and offer him the chance to marry a bride of the greatest beauty."

The Cloud was rather surprised when Mr and Mrs Rat called on him to offer him their daughter's hand in marriage. He agreed with them that she was indeed a most beautiful rat, but he did not like the idea of marrying her at all. He considered carefully before replying.

"My friend the Sun is kind to describe me as the most powerful thing in the world but I'm afraid he's mistaken. The Wind is far more powerful than I am. The Wind can blow me across the sky at a moment's notice. I think you should call on the Wind and suggest he marries your daughter."

Mr and Mrs Rat saw at once that what the Cloud said was true so they took their daughter to visit the Wind.

The Wind stopped blowing for a few minutes to talk to the Rat family, but he did not like the idea of marrying at all. He was far too busy to stay still in one place for long, even for a few minutes.

So the Wind said to Mr and Mrs Rat:

"The Cloud was right to say I am more powerful than he, but have you considered that the Wall over there is more powerful than me? However hard I blow, I can never blow him down. I think you should take your beautiful daughter to him. He is the most powerful of all."

The Wind rushed off, leaving Mr and Mrs Rat nodding at his wisdom. "Come along child," they said to their daughter. "We will go and see the Wall. He will surely be glad to have such a beautiful bride."

When they arrived at the Wall, Mr and Mrs Rat bowed low before him, for they could see he was extremely strong and powerful. They explained that they had come to offer him their beautiful daughter as a wife and the Wall replied that he would think over the idea very carefully. But while he was thinking, there was a sudden and unexpected interruption.

"I don't want to marry a Wall," shouted Miss Rat, twitching her whiskers and stamping her foot. "I would have married the Sun, or the Cloud, or the Wind, but I don't want to have a Wall for my husband," and she burst into tears.

Mr and Mrs Rat were horrified at their daughter's rudeness, but the Wall said with great tact, "Your daughter is right. She should not marry me. There is only one animal who can reduce me, a Wall, into dust. That animal is the rat, who can gnaw through me with his sharp teeth. I would advise you to marry your daughter to the finest rat you can find. She will never have a more powerful husband."

And so it ended happily. Mr Rat was glad because he had always thought there was no finer creature on earth than the rat. Mrs Rat was pleased now that she knew how powerful a rat husband would be. As for the Rats' Daughter, she thought she would be very happy indeed married to a handsome young rat.

OLD MOTHER GOOSE

Old Mother Goose,
  When she wanted to wander,
Would ride through the air
  On a very fine gander.

Mother Goose had a house,
  'Twas built in a wood,
Where an owl at the door
  For sentinel stood.

She had a son Jack,
  A plain-looking lad,
He was not very good,
  Nor yet very bad.

She sent him to market,
  A live goose he bought;
See, mother, says he,
  I have not been for naught.

Jack's goose and her gander
  Grew very fond;
They'd both eat together,
  Or swim in the pond.

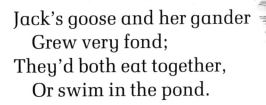

Jack found one fine morning,
As I have been told,
His goose had laid him
An egg of pure gold.

Jack ran to his mother
The news for to tell.
She called him a good boy
And said it was well.

Jack sold his gold egg
To a merchant untrue,
Who cheated him out of
A half of his due.

Then Jack went a-courting
    A lady so gay,
As fair as the lily,
    And sweet as the May.

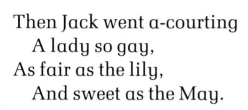

The merchant and squire
    Soon came at his back
And began to belabour
    The sides of poor Jack.

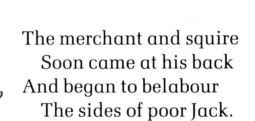

Then old Mother Goose
    That instant came in,
And turned her son Jack
    Into famed Harlequin.

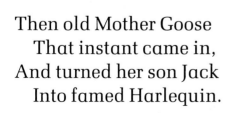

Pegasus the Winged Horse

Long, long ago, there lived the fiercest monster imaginable, called the Chimera. He had three heads, each of them different, and could breathe fire from all three mouths at once. One head was shaped like a goat, one like a lion, and the third was in the form of a serpent. All might have been well if the monster had lived quietly in the mountains, but he was forever coming down into the cities and villages, eating people, destroying buildings and burning up crops o 1 the farms. No one could get near enough to kill him and it looked as though the whole of the country would be destroyed by the Chimera.

The king of this land offered a great reward to anyone who would rid him of the Chimera. There was a young man called Bellerophon, who wanted to prove his bravery, and so he came forward. He had an idea that if he could attack the monster from the air he might have a chance of winning.

One night, in a dream, Athene, the Goddess of Wisdom, came to Bellerophon and told him about Pegasus, the winged horse of the gods, of the fountain where the horse liked to drink, and where he might find a golden bridle which would help him tame the horse. After a long journey Bellerophon reached the fountain and found the bridle of gold. He hid until Pegasus came to drink, then crept up and slipped the bridle over the horse's neck.

Pegasus, who had never been touched by a man before,

jumped away, and as he did so Bellerophon leapt onto his back. A great struggle then took place between them for Pegasus tried every trick he knew to throw Bellerophon. He soared up into the sky; he twisted, bucked, reared, spun round. Somehow Bellerophon hung on, and at last he was able to get the bit into Pegasus's mouth. Soon after this Pegasus gave in and came to rest on the ground, his sides heaving with exhaustion.

Bellerophon explained to the beautiful white winged horse why he had captured him, and how he needed his help to save the kingdom from the fire-eating monster. As he spoke, he saw that there were tears in the horse's eyes, and said, "I cannot do this to you. It is no quarrel of yours. You shall go free and I must find some other way to win this victory." He took off the bridle and watched Pegasus soar into the sky.

In a few minutes, just as he was about to start his journey home, he felt a gentle nuzzle by his arm. To Bellerophon's delight the horse had returned of his own free will.

For many days they trained together so that they would have the best possible chance against the Chimera. At last, the day came. Bellerophon took out his finest armour, sharpened his sword and flew off on Pegasus's back to seek the monster.

The Chimera was outside his cave, preparing to raid another village. Before he knew what was happening, and without hearing more than a faint whirr in the air above him, he felt an agonizing blow. Bellerophon had chopped off one of his heads. It was the goat's head, and it lay in the dust while the monster roared with pain and lashed his tail with rage. Smoke and flames shot out in every direction as he tried to find his attacker.

Hidden by the smoke, Pegasus and Bellerophon were able to swoop down on him again and in a flash the sword swept through another neck. This time the lion's head rolled in the dust. The monster was wild and savage with pain and anger. He hurled himself at his attackers, and clung to Pegasus with his huge scaly claws as the horse rose into the air. Bellerophon thought they would surely die; the heat from the flames was terrible, and the serpent's head was only inches from his own. But the horse never wavered, soaring higher and higher into the air.

As the serpent's head stretched out to strike, Bellerophon saw a weak spot under its neck and drove his sword in with all his strength. The Chimera gave a ghastly scream. His hold on Pegasus loosened and he tumbled backwards in a shower of sparks. He crashed to the ground burning as he went.

Bellerophon became a great hero, and so did the winged horse. They had other adventures together, but when Bellerophon tried to fly to heaven with Pegasus he was thrown. Some people said that Zeus, the king of the gods, was jealous, and sent an insect to tickle Pegasus and make him throw his rider. Pegasus went on flying up to heaven where he was changed into a group of stars, which you may see shining in the sky on a clear night.

POLLY FLINDERS

Little Polly Flinders
Sat among the cinders,
Warming her pretty little toes;
Her mother came and caught her,
And whipped her little daughter
For spoiling her nice new clothes.

MY FATHER DIED

My father died a month ago
    And left me all his riches;
A feather bed, a wooden leg,
    And a pair of leather breeches;
A coffee pot without a spout,
    A cup without a handle,
A tobacco pipe without a lid,
    And half a farthing candle.

THE NORTH WIND

The north wind doth blow,
And we shall have snow,
And what will poor Robin do then,
   Poor thing?
He'll sit in a barn,
And keep himself warm,
And hide his head under his wing,
   Poor thing.

THE BEGGARS

Hark, hark, the dogs do bark,
   The beggars are coming to town;
Some in rags and some in tags,
   And one in a velvet gown.

THREE LITTLE KITTENS

Three little kittens
They lost their mittens,
   And they began to cry,
Oh, Mother dear,
We sadly fear
Our mittens we have lost.
What! lost your mittens,
You naughty kittens!
Then you shall have no pie.
   Mee-ow, mee-ow, mee-ow.
No, you shall have no pie.

The three little kittens
They found their mittens,
   And they began to cry,
Oh, Mother dear,
See here, see here,
Our mittens we have found.
Put on your mittens,
You silly kittens,
And you shall have some pie.
   Purr-r, purr-r, purr-r,
Oh, let us have some pie.

The three little kittens
Put on their mittens
   And soon ate up the pie;
Oh, Mother dear,
We greatly fear
Our mittens we have soiled.
What! soiled your mittens,
You naughty kittens!
Then they began to sigh,
   Mee-ow, mee-ow, mee-ow,
Then they began to sigh.

The three little kittens
They washed their mittens,
   And hung them out to dry;
Oh, Mother dear,
Do you not hear,
Our mittens we have washed.
What! washed your mittens,
You good little kittens,
But I smell a rat close by.
   Mee-ow, mee-ow, mee-ow,
We smell a rat close by.

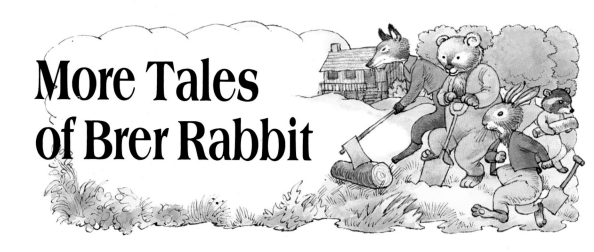

More Tales of Brer Rabbit

One hot summer's day Brer Rabbit, Brer Fox and the other animals were clearing some ground so that it could be planted for the next year. The sun got hot and Brer Rabbit got tired. By and by he hollered out that he had a thorn in his hand and he slipped off to find a cool place to rest. He came across a well with two buckets hanging over it.

"That looks cool," says Brer Rabbit to himself. "I'll just get in there and take a nap." And with that, in he jumped.

He was no sooner in the bucket than it began to drop down the well. There has never been a more scared creature than Brer Rabbit at that moment. Suddenly he felt the bucket hit the water. And Brer Rabbit, he kept as still as he could and just lay there and shook and shivered.

Now Brer Fox always had one eye on Brer Rabbit, and when he slipped off Brer Fox sneaked after him. He knew Brer Rabbit was up to something. Brer Fox saw Brer Rabbit go to the well, jump in the bucket and disappear out of sight.

Brer Fox was the most astonished fox that you ever laid eyes on. He sat there in the bushes and thought and thought and thought but could not make head nor tail of what was going on.

Then he said to himself, "Right down in that well is where Brer Rabbit keeps his money hidden. If that's not it, then he's discovered a gold mine. I'm going to find out."

Brer Fox crept a little nearer, but he heard nothing. So he crept a little nearer again and still heard nothing. Then he got right up close and peered down into the well.

All this time Brer Rabbit was lying in the bucket scared out of his skin. If he moved the bucket might tip over and spill him out into the water. As he was saying his prayers, old Brer Fox hollered out,

"Heyo, Brer Rabbit, who are you visiting down there?"

"Who? Me? Oh, I'm just fishing, Brer Fox," says Brer Rabbit. "I just said to myself I'd sort of surprise you with a lot of fishes for dinner, so here I am, and here are all the fishes. I'm fishing for suckers, Brer Fox," says Brer Rabbit.

"Are there many down there, Brer Rabbit?" says Brer Fox.

"Lots of them, Brer Fox. Scores and scores of them. The water is alive with them. Come down and help me haul them in."

"How am I going to get down, Brer Rabbit?"

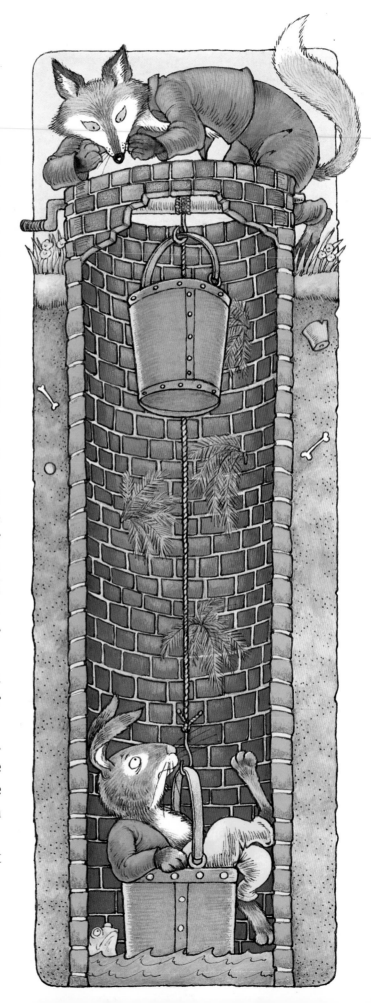

"Jump into the bucket, Brer Fox. It will bring you down safe and sound."

Brer Rabbit sounded so happy that Brer Fox jumped into the other bucket and it began to fall. As he went down into the well, his weight pulled Brer Rabbit's bucket up. When they passed one another, half-way up and half-way down, Brer Rabbit called out,

> "Goodbye, Brer Fox, take care of your clothes,
> For this is the way the world goes,
> Some goes up and some goes down,
> You'll get to the bottom safe and sound."

Brer Rabbit's bucket reached the top of the well and he jumped out. He galloped off to the people who owned the well and told them that Brer Fox was down in the well muddying their drinking water. Then he galloped back to the well and hollered down to Brer Fox,

> "Here comes a man with a great big gun,
> When he hauls you up, you jump and run."

Well, in about half an hour both of them were back on the ground that was being cleared, working as though they'd never heard of any well, except every now and then Brer Rabbit burst out laughing. And Brer Fox, he looked mighty sore.

Now this is how Brer Fox got his revenge. One day he got some tar, mixed it with some turpentine and fixed up a contraption which he called a Tar-Baby. He took this Tar-Baby and he sat her in the middle of the road and then he lay in the bushes to see what was going to happen.

Brer Fox did not have to wait long because by and by along came Brer Rabbit all dressed up as fine as a jaybird. *Lippity-clippity clippity-lippity*, Brer Rabbit pranced along until he spied the Tar-Baby. He stopped in astonishment.

"Morning!" says Brer Rabbit. "Nice weather this morning!" he says. But the Tar-Baby said nothing and Brer Fox, he lay low.

"Are you deaf?" says Brer Rabbit, "for if you are, I can holler louder." And he hollers, "Can you hear me now?"

The Tar-Baby stayed still and Brer Fox, he lay low.

"You're stuck up, that's what you are," shouts Brer Rabbit. "I'm going to teach you how to talk to respectable folks. If you don't take that hat off, I'll hit you."

But of course the Tar-Baby stayed still and Brer Fox, he lay low. Brer Rabbit drew back his fist and *blip*, he hit the side of the Tar-Baby's head. His fist stuck and he couldn't pull loose.

"If you don't let me loose I'll hit you again," says Brer Rabbit, and he swiped at the Tar-Baby with his other hand and that stuck too.

"Let me loose before I kick the stuffing out of you," hollers Brer Rabbit.

But the Tar-Baby said nothing. She just held on and Brer Rabbit soon found his feet stuck in the same way. Then he butted the Tar-Baby with his head and that stuck too.

Now Brer Fox sauntered out of the bushes, looking as innocent as a mocking-bird.

"Howdy, Brer Rabbit," he says, "you look sort of stuck up this morning," and he rolled on the ground with laughter.

As Brer Rabbit struggled on the ground with the Tar-Baby, Brer Fox crowed triumphantly,

"Hah! I've got you this time and it's your own fault. No one asked you to strike up an acquaintance with the Tar-Baby. You just stuck yourself on to it, and now I'm going to make a fire and barbecue you."

Then Brer Rabbit began to talk in a very humble voice.

"I don't care what you do to me," he says, "as long as you don't throw me in that briar patch."

"It's so much trouble to kindle a fire, I think I'll hang you or drown you instead," says Brer Fox.

"Hang me as high as you please, drown me as deep as you please, Brer Fox, but don't fling me in that briar patch."

Now Brer Fox wanted to hurt Brer Rabbit as much as possible, so he picked him up by the hind legs and slung him right into the middle of the briar patch. With that, Brer Fox turned his back on Brer Rabbit and sauntered off down the road, looking mighty pleased with himself.

Suddenly he heard someone calling him. Way up the hill was Brer Rabbit sitting cross-legged on a log, combing tar out of his fur. Then Brer Fox knew he'd been tricked, and just to rub it in Brer Rabbit called out,

"Bred and born in a briar patch, Brer Fox, bred and born in a briar patch."

With that, he skipped off as lively as a cricket and lived to trick Brer Fox another day.

THE HOUSE THAT JACK BUILT

This is the house
  that Jack built.

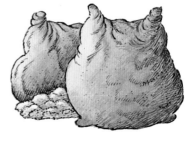

This is the malt
That lay in the house
  that Jack built.

This is the rat
That ate the malt
That lay in the house
  that Jack built.

This is the cat
That killed the rat
That ate the malt
That lay in the house
  that Jack built.

This is the dog
That worried the cat
That killed the rat
That ate the malt
That lay in the house
  that Jack built.

This is the cow
   with the crumpled horn,
That tossed the dog
That worried the cat
That killed the rat
That ate the malt
That lay in the house
   that Jack built.

This is the maiden all forlorn,
That milked the cow
   with the crumpled horn,
That tossed the dog
That worried the cat
That killed the rat
That ate the malt
That lay in the house
   that Jack built.

This is the man all tattered
    and torn,
That kissed the maiden
    all forlorn,
That milked the cow
    with the crumpled horn,
That tossed the dog
That worried the cat
That killed the rat
That ate the malt
That lay in the house
    that Jack built.

This is the priest all shaven and shorn,
That married the man
    all tattered and torn,
That kissed the maiden all forlorn,
That milked the cow
    with the crumpled horn,
That tossed the dog
That worried the cat
That killed the rat
That ate the malt
That lay in the house
    that Jack built.

This is the cock
   that crowed in the morn,
That waked the priest
   all shaven and shorn,
That married the man
   all tattered and torn,
That kissed the maiden
   all forlorn,
That milked the cow
   with the crumpled horn,
That tossed the dog
That worried the cat
That killed the rat
That ate the malt
That lay in the house
   that Jack built.

This is the farmer sowing his corn,
That kept the cock that crowed in the morn,
That waked the priest all shaven and shorn,
That married the man all tattered and torn,
That kissed the maiden all forlorn,
That milked the cow with
    the crumpled horn,
That tossed the dog
That worried the cat
That killed the rat
That ate the malt
That lay in the house
    that Jack built.

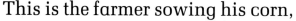

This is the horse and the hound and the horn,
That belonged to the farmer sowing his corn,
That kept the cock that crowed in the morn,
That waked the priest all shaven and shorn,
That married the man all tattered and torn,
That kissed the maiden all forlorn,
            That milked the cow with
                the crumpled horn,
            That tossed the dog
            That worried the cat
            That killed the rat
            That ate the malt
            That lay in the house
                that Jack built.

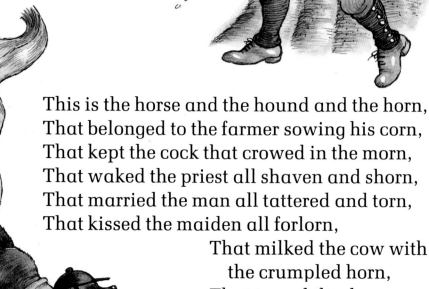

The Tinder Box

A soldier was marching along the road on his way home from
the wars one day when an old woman came out from behind a
tree and stopped him. She was as ugly as a witch but she seemed
friendly enough as she admired the soldier's sword.

"How would you like to take home with you as much money
as you can carry, soldier?" she asked.

"I'd like it a lot," he said, "only where can I find the money,
old woman?"

"Listen and I'll tell you," the witch woman replied. "If you
climb into this tree, you will find it is hollow. Go down inside it
and you will find yourself in a deep shaft. At the bottom there is a
passage and you will see three doors.

"The first door leads to a room guarded by a fierce dog with
eyes as big as tea cups. In it you will find as much bronze money
as you could want. Take this apron of mine and spread it out on
the floor. If the dog sits on it he will do you no harm. But if you
prefer it, go on to the second door."

"What shall I find there?" interrupted the soldier.

"Ah!" said the old woman. "There you will find as much
silver as you can carry, and more. But this room is guarded by a
dog whose eyes are as big as mill wheels. He too is fierce, but will
not hurt you once he has sat on my apron.

"In the last room you will find gold coins, masses and
masses of gold coins, but take care here, for the dog that guards the
gold has eyes as big as towers. He is even fiercer, but he too will not
hurt you if he sits on my apron."

"It all sounds very good, old woman," said the soldier

cheerfully, "but what are you going to get out of it? I can't believe you would give me this chance to get rich without wanting a favour of some kind yourself."

"Quite right, soldier," she replied. "You must bring me the tinder box that lies on the table at the end of the passage. My grandmother gave it to me, but I forgot to bring it up last time I was down there. I'm too old now to climb down the shaft to fetch it. Tie this rope round your waist so that I can help pull you up when you have finished."

The soldier tied the rope round his waist and climbed into the hollow tree. It was just as the old woman had described and the soldier clambered down a long shaft deep into the ground, and found himself in a passage. It was lit by many candles so he could see the three doors quite clearly.

He opened the first door and gasped with pleasure. There before him were chests and chests of bronze money but standing in front of them was a fierce-looking dog with eyes as big as tea cups. The soldier whistled cheerfully and laid the apron on the floor.

To his relief the dog sat on the apron and the soldier went over to the chests and stuffed his pockets with the bronze money. Then he picked up the apron and returned to the passage.

The soldier went on to the second door, and when he peeped inside he saw an even fiercer dog with eyes as big as mill wheels. Behind him were caskets full of silver. The greedy soldier put the witch's apron on the ground and as soon as the dog was sitting on it, he emptied all the bronze money out of his pockets, picked up handfuls of silver coins and filled his pockets and his knapsack. He was so weighed down when he left the room he could scarcely pick up the witch's apron. He then staggered on down the passage to the third door.

Inside, the whole room seemed to sparkle from the gold the soldier could see, but between him and the gold stood the fiercest-looking dog he had ever seen with eyes as big as towers. The soldier spread the apron on the floor very carefully and to his relief the dog sat on it. The soldier quickly threw out all the silver he had collected, and picked up gold coins as fast as he could, cramming them into his pockets, his knapsack and even his hat.

The soldier went back to the shaft to climb up into the hollow tree. He tugged at the rope so the old woman could help him, but she called down:

"Did you get my tinder box, soldier?"

"Why no, I forgot!" called back the soldier. "I'll get it now."

He went back along the passage and found the tinder box where she had said it would be, and he picked it up and returned to the bottom of the shaft.

As soon as he was out of the hollow tree the soldier asked the old woman why the tinder box was so important to her but she would not tell him. "If you don't answer me," he shouted, "I shall cut off your head with my fine sword," but the old woman just held out her hand for the tinder box. The soldier, who was used to getting his own way, drew his sword and with one swift stroke he chopped off her head.

The soldier went on his way cheerfully, and in the evening he came to a big town and took rooms in the best inn. The innkeeper was surprised that a mere soldier wanted such an expensive room, and the boot boy wondered at the shabby old boots put out to be cleaned, but they said nothing, for they had seen the gleam of gold in the soldier's hand.

The next day, the soldier went out and bought himself fine clothes and new boots. For many months he stayed in the inn, and lived like a rich gentleman. He made many friends and gave wild expensive parties. Each day his supply of gold got less until the day came when he had nothing at all.

Now the soldier had to move into a small dismal attic room. His new friends disappeared and the soldier found himself alone and cold and hungry. One dark night as he sat huddled in a chair he caught sight of an old candle stub. It was all he had left to give him a few moments of warmth and light. Remembering the old woman's tinder box, he struck it once to light the candle. To his amazement he saw the dog with eyes as big as tea cups in the room with him.

"What do you want, master?" the dog asked. "Shall I fetch you some money?" and even as the soldier nodded the dog disappeared and returned with a bag of bronze coins in his mouth.

The soldier struck the tinder box twice and the dog with eyes as big as mill wheels was there, saying, "What do you want, master?" and he too disappeared and came back with a bag of money, but this time it was in silver coins. The soldier struck the tinder box again three times, and there was the huge dog with eyes as big as towers. In a flash, he too disappeared and returned with a bag of gold coins.

"Now I know why the old woman was so anxious to get this tinder box," said the soldier, smiling to himself.

The next day he moved to fine lodgings and all his friends came to see him again, and the parties started once more. The soldier seemed to have everything he could want, but there was one thing he could not do, and this annoyed him very much. At the end of the town was the king's palace, and it was said the king had a most beautiful daughter. The soldier longed to see her but his friends told him it was impossible.

"No one is allowed to see her," they said. "The king was once told that she would marry a common soldier so now he keeps her in the palace where she will never meet anyone but a prince."

The soldier often thought about the princess and wondered how he could arrange to see her. One night he had an idea. He struck the tinder box once and when the dog with eyes as big as tea cups appeared, he did not ask for money as he usually did, but told the dog he wished to see the princess. In no time at all the dog

returned carrying the sleeping princess on its back. The soldier found her extremely beautiful and made up his mind that each night one of the dogs should bring the princess to him.

One morning the princess told her parents of a dream she often had. "It is a strange dream," she said. "A huge dog with enormous eyes appears and carries me into the town and then to a room where there is a fine rich gentleman."

The king and queen were worried and asked one of the ladies-in-waiting to watch the princess during the night. That night the lady-in-waiting kept watch and saw a great dog with eyes as big as mill wheels carry the princess away on its back. Quickly she followed them through the town to the house where the dog took the princess. Then she made a cross on the door with chalk. But the dog saw her and, after he had returned the princess to the palace, he put chalk crosses on all the doors in the town.

The next day the king and queen, led by the lady-in-waiting, set out to find the scoundrel who sent his dog each night to fetch their daughter, but as they found each door marked with a cross

they were completely confused. The queen was determined to find
out what happened to their daughter each night, so she made
another plan. She filled a little silk bag with fine flour, snipped a
small hole in the corner and tied this to her daughter before she
went to bed.

   The next morning she and the king were able to follow the
trail of flour to the soldier's lodgings. Immediately the king had the
soldier thrown into prison, and announced that he would be
executed the next day.

   As the soldier sat in his cell waiting for death, a boy outside
tripped and lost his shoe through the cell grating. "If you want it
back," called the soldier, "go to my lodgings and bring me my
tinder box. I'll give you four pence too." The boy went willingly to
fetch the tinder box for he was glad to earn four pence.

A large crowd gathered to see the soldier executed. As he climbed the scaffold the soldier asked for one last wish.

"Let me smoke my pipe one last time before I die," he said.

"Very well, soldier," said the king. "Your wish is granted."

The soldier took out his tinder box. He struck it once, then twice, then three times.

Immediately the three huge dogs appeared and their master shouted, "Save me!"

The dogs bounded forward and the king and queen and all the guards were slain. Most of the crowd ran away, but those who stayed decided that the soldier should be their new king. They could see he was very powerful!

The soldier gladly accepted and the first thing he did was to marry the beautiful princess. They lived together in the palace and the soldier always had everything he wanted, for the dog with eyes as big as tea cups, the dog with eyes as big as mill wheels and the dog with eyes as big as towers were always there to carry out his orders. And from that day onwards, the soldier was careful to carry the tinder box with him wherever he went.

THE GRAND OLD DUKE
OF YORK

Oh, the grand old Duke of York,
   He had ten thousand men;
He marched them up to the top of the hill,
   And he marched them down again.
And when they were up, they were up,
   And when they were down, they were down,
And when they were only halfway up,
   They were neither up nor down.

THIS LITTLE PIG

This little pig went to market;
This little pig stayed at home;

This little pig had roast beef;
This little pig had none;
And this little pig cried, Wee-wee-wee!
   All the way home.

The Old Woman and her Pig

There was once an old woman who found some money under the floorboards of her house. "How lucky I am," she said. "I can go to the market and buy myself a pig."

So the old woman went to the market and bought herself a fine pig. Now it's easy to take a pig home from market if you have a lorry or truck, or even a cart, but the old woman had none of these and so she had to walk home with the pig.

On the way she decided to take a short cut through the fields. But she had forgotten that there was a stile between two fields on her way and now, however hard she tried, the old woman could not make the pig climb over the stile.

The old woman saw a dog so she said:
"Dog! Dog! Bite the pig!
The pig won't climb over the stile,
and I shan't get home tonight!"
But the dog would not bite the pig.

Then the old woman saw a stick, and she said:
"Stick! Stick! Beat the dog!
The dog won't bite the pig,
The pig won't climb over the stile,
and I shan't get home tonight!"
But the stick would not beat the dog.

The old woman went a little farther and she found a fire, and she said:
"Fire! Fire! Burn the stick!
The stick won't beat the dog,
The dog won't bite the pig,
The pig won't climb over the stile,
and I shan't get home tonight!"

But the fire would not burn the stick.

The old woman was getting very cross wondering how she was ever going to get the pig over the stile, when she saw a bucket of water. So she said:

"Water! Water! Put out the fire!
The fire won't burn the stick,
The stick won't beat the dog,
The dog won't bite the pig,
The pig won't climb over the stile,
and I shan't get home tonight!"

But the water would not put out the fire.

The old woman went a little farther and she saw a bull standing in the field. So she said:

"Bull! Bull! Drink the water!
The water won't put out the fire,
The fire won't burn the stick,
The stick won't beat the dog,
The dog won't bite the pig,
The pig won't climb over the stile,
and I shan't get home tonight!"

But the bull would not drink the water.

The old woman went a little farther and met a butcher. So she said:

"Butcher! Butcher! Kill the bull!
The bull won't drink the water,
The water won't put out the fire,
The fire won't burn the stick,
The stick won't beat the dog,
The dog won't bite the pig,
The pig won't climb over the stile,
and I shan't get home tonight!"

But the butcher would not kill the bull.

The old woman went a little farther and saw a rope, and she said:

"Rope! Rope! Hang the butcher!
The butcher won't kill the bull,
The bull won't drink the water,
The water won't put out the fire,
The fire won't burn the stick,
The stick won't beat the dog,
The dog won't bite the pig,
The pig won't climb over the stile,
and I shan't get home tonight!"

But the rope would not hang the butcher.

Then the old woman went a little farther and caught sight of a rat, and she said:

"Rat! Rat! Gnaw the rope!
The rope won't hang the butcher,
The butcher won't kill the bull,
The bull won't drink the water,
The water won't put out the fire,
The fire won't burn the stick,
The stick won't beat the dog,
The dog won't bite the pig,
The pig won't climb over the stile,
and I shan't get home tonight!"

But the rat would not gnaw the rope.

The old woman wondered what on earth she was going to do when she saw a cat, and she said:

"Cat! Cat! Catch the rat!
The rat won't gnaw the rope,
The rope won't hang the butcher,
The butcher won't kill the bull,
The bull won't drink the water,
The water won't put out the fire,
The fire won't burn the stick,
The stick won't beat the dog,
The dog won't bite the pig,
The pig won't climb over the stile,
and I shan't get home tonight!"

The cat said, "If you bring me a saucer of milk I will catch the rat for you."

The old woman jumped for joy and ran over to a cow in the next field, crying, "Cow! Cow! Will you give me some milk for the cat?" and the cow said:

"If you bring me some hay from that haystack over there I will give you some milk."

So the old woman fetched some hay for the cow and the cow let the old woman milk her. She took the milk to the cat and the cat lapped it up.

Then the cat began to chase the rat,
The rat began to gnaw the rope,
The rope began to hang the butcher,
The butcher began to kill the bull,
The bull began to drink the water,
The water began to put out the fire,
The fire began to burn the stick,
The stick began to beat the dog,
The dog began to bite the pig,
The pig got a tremendous fright and leapt over the stile and the old lady got home that night.

WHERE, OH WHERE

Oh, where, oh, where has my little dog gone?
    Oh where, oh, where can he be?
With his ears cut short and his tail cut long,
    Oh, where, oh, where is he?

A MAN OF THESSALY

There was a man of Thessaly
    And he was wondrous wise,
He jumped into a bramble bush
    And scratched out both his eyes.
And when he saw his eyes were out,
    With all his might and main
He jumped into another bush
    And scratched them in again.

BANDY LEGS

As I was going to sell my eggs
I met a man with bandy legs,
Bandy legs and crooked toes;
I tripped up his heels, and he fell on his nose.

HOT CROSS BUNS

Hot cross buns! Hot cross buns!
One a penny, two a penny,
Hot cross buns!
If you have no daughters
Give them to your sons;
One a penny, two a penny,
Hot cross buns.

THE LITTLE NUT TREE

I had a little nut tree,
    Nothing would it bear
But a silver nutmeg
    And a golden pear.
The king of Spain's daughter
    Came to visit me,
All for the sake
    Of my little nut tree.

DIDDLE, DIDDLE, DUMPLING

Diddle, diddle, dumpling, my son John,
Went to bed with his trousers on;
One shoe off, and one shoe on,
Diddle, diddle, dumpling, my son John.

TWINKLE, TWINKLE

Twinkle, twinkle, little star,
How I wonder what you are!
Up above the world so high,
Like a diamond in the sky.

THE KEY OF THE KINGDOM

This is the key of the kingdom.
In that kingdom is a city,
In that city is a town,
In that town there is a street,
In that street there winds a lane,
In that lane there is a yard,
In that yard there is a house,
In that house there waits a room,
In that room there is a bed,
On that bed there is a basket,
    A basket of flowers.

Flowers in the basket,
Basket on the bed,
Bed in the chamber,
Chamber in the house,
House in the weedy yard,
Yard in the winding lane,
Lane in the broad street,
Street in the high town,
Town in the city,
City in the kingdom:
    This is the key of the kingdom.

Aladdin and his Wonderful Lamp

Far off in a beautiful city in China a ragged urchin called Aladdin used to play in the street. His father, a poor tailor, tried to make him work, but Aladdin was lazy and disobedient, and refused even to help in his father's shop. Even after his father died Aladdin still preferred to roam in the streets with his friends, and did not feel ashamed to eat the food his mother bought with the money she earned by spinning cotton.

One day a wealthy stranger came to the city. He noticed Aladdin in the street and thought, "That lad looks as though he has no purpose in life. It will not matter if I use him, then kill him."

The stranger quickly found out that Aladdin's father, Mustapha, was now dead. He called Aladdin over to him.

"Greetings, nephew," he said, "I am your father's brother. I have returned to China only to find my dear brother, Mustapha, is dead. Take this money and tell your mother I shall visit her."

Aladdin's mother was puzzled when Aladdin told her the stranger's message. "You have no uncle," she said. "I don't understand why this man should give us money."

The next day the stranger came to their house and talked about how he had loved his brother and offered to buy a fine shop where Aladdin could sell beautiful things to the rich people in the city. He gave Aladdin some new clothes and in a short while Aladdin's mother began to believe this man was a relation.

The stranger now invited Aladdin to go with him to the rich part of the city. Together they walked through beautiful gardens

and parks where Aladdin had never been before, until he found himself far from home. At last the stranger showed Aladdin a flat stone with an iron ring set into it.

"Lift this stone for me, nephew," he said, "and go into the cavern below. Walk through three caves where you will see gold and silver stored. Do not touch it. You will then pass through a garden full of wonderful fruit and beyond the trees you will find a lamp. Pour out the oil and bring the lamp to me. Pick some of the fruit on your return if you wish."

Aladdin lifted the stone and saw some steps leading down into a cave. He was frightened to go down but the stranger placed a gold ring with a great green emerald on his finger.

"Take this ring as a gift," he said, "but you must go or I shall not buy you a shop."

Now the stranger was in fact a magician. He had read about a lamp with magical powers and he had travelled far to find it. He knew the magic would not work for him unless the lamp was fetched from the cavern and handed to him by someone else. After Aladdin had brought him the lamp the magician planned to shut him in the cave to die.

Down in the cavern Aladdin found all as he had been told. He hurried through the rooms filled with silver and gold, and passed through the garden where the trees were hung with shimmering fruit of all colours. At the far end stood an old lamp. Aladdin took it, poured out the oil, and then picked some of the

dazzling fruit from the trees as the magician had suggested. To his surprise they were all made from stones. Aladdin took as many as he could carry and returned to the steps.

"Give me the lamp," demanded the magician as soon as Aladdin came into sight.

"Help me out first," replied Aladdin who could not hand him the lamp because his arms were so full. They argued fiercely until crash, the stone slab fell back into place. The magician could not move the stone from the outside, nor Aladdin from within. He was trapped. The magician knew he had failed in his quest and decided to leave the country at once.

For two days Aladdin tried to get out of the cave. He became weak with hunger and thirst and finally as he sat in despair he rubbed his hands together. By chance he rubbed the gold ring that the stranger had given him. There was a blinding flash and a genie appeared. "I am the genie of the ring. What can I do for you, master?" it said.

"Get me out of here," Aladdin gasped. He was terrified of the great burning spirit of the genie glowing in the cavern. Before he knew what had happened he was standing on the ground above the entrance to the cavern. Of the stone slab there was no sign. Aladdin set off for home and collapsed with hunger as he entered the house.

His mother was overjoyed to see him. She gave him all the scraps of food she had and when she said she had no more Aladdin suggested selling the lamp to buy some food.

"I'll get a better price for it, if it's clean," she thought, and she rubbed the lamp with a cloth. In a flash the genie appeared. Aladdin's mother fainted in horror but Aladdin seized the lamp. When the genie saw him with the lamp it said:

"I am the genie of the lamp. What can I do for you, master?"

"Get me some food," ordered Aladdin.

By the time his mother had recovered there were twelve silver dishes of food and twelve silver cups on the table. Aladdin and his mother ate as they had never eaten before. They had enough for several days, and then Aladdin began to sell the silver dishes and cups. He and his mother lived comfortably in this way for some time.

Then it happened that Aladdin saw the sultan's daughter, Princess Badroulboudoir. Aladdin loved her at first sight and sent his mother to the sultan's court to ask the sultan's permission for the princess to marry him. He told her to take as a gift the stone fruits he had brought from the cave.

It was several days before Aladdin's mother could speak with the sultan, but at last she was able to give him the stone fruits. The sultan was truly amazed.

"Your son has such fine jewels he would make a good husband for my daughter, I am sure," he told Aladdin's mother.

But the sultan's chief courtier was jealous. He wanted his son to marry the princess. Quickly, he advised the sultan to say he would decide on the marriage in three months time. Aladdin was happy when he heard the news. He felt sure he would marry the princess in three months time.

But at the palace, the chief courtier spoke against Aladdin and when Aladdin's mother returned in three months, the sultan asked her:

"Can your son send me forty golden bowls full of jewels like the ones he sent before only this time carried by forty servants?"

Aladdin rubbed the lamp once more and before long forty servants each carrying a gold bowl filled with sparkling jewels

were assembled in the courtyard of their little house.

When the sultan saw them, he said:

"I am sure now that the owner of these riches will make a fine husband for my daughter."

But the chief courtier suggested yet another test. "Ask the woman," he said, "if her son has a palace fit for your daughter to live in."

"I'll give him the land and he can build a new palace," declared the sultan, and he presented Aladdin with land in front of his own palace.

Aladdin summoned the genie of the lamp once more. Overnight the most amazing palace appeared with walls of gold and silver, huge windows, beautiful halls and courtyards and rooms filled with treasures. A carpet of red velvet was laid from the old palace to the new, for the princess to walk on to her new home. Aladdin then asked the genie for some fine clothes for himself and his mother, and a glorious wedding took place with a splendid banquet eaten off golden dishes.

Aladdin took care always to keep the wonderful lamp safe. One day the princess gave it to an old beggar who was the magician in disguise, but that story, and the story of how Aladdin got it back again, will have to keep for another time.

THE PIE

Who made the pie?
I did.

Who stole the pie?
He did.

Who found the pie?
She did.

Who ate the pie?
You did.

Who cried for pie?
We all did.

PETER, PETER

Peter, Peter, pumpkin eater,
Had a wife and couldn't keep her;
He put her in a pumpkin shell,
And there he kept her very well.

MY BLACK HEN

Hickety, pickety, my black hen,
She lays eggs for gentlemen;
Sometimes one, and sometimes ten,
Hickety, pickety, my black hen.

THREE YOUNG RATS

Three young rats with black felt hats,
Three young ducks with new straw flats,
Three young dogs with curling tails,
Three young cats with demi-veils,
Went out to walk with two young pigs
In satin vests and sorrel wigs;
But suddenly it chanced to rain
And so they all went home again.

TERENCE
McDIDDLER

Terence McDiddler,
The three-stringed fiddler,
Can charm, if you please,
The fish from the seas.

The Travelling Musicians

One day an old donkey overheard his master saying that he was too old for work. The time had come for him to be killed off for they could not keep an animal who was no longer useful.

"Killed indeed!" snorted the donkey. "I may be too old to carry heavy loads but I am not too old to make a fine noise when I bray. I shall go to the neighbouring town of Bremen and earn my keep there as a musician."

He unlatched the stable door with his teeth, a trick he had learned long ago, and when no one was looking he slipped out and trotted down the road towards Bremen.

He had not gone far when he saw an old dog lying by the side of the road looking rather sorry for himself.

"Why so sad, Dog?" he asked.

"You would feel just as sad if you had overheard your master say he was going to knock you on the head because you were too old."

"Come with me, friend," said the donkey. "I am also too old for my master, so I am off to Bremen to earn my living as a musician. You can use your voice, can't you? Together we will sing a fine duet."

The dog agreed to travel to Bremen with the donkey, and they trotted down the road together. Before long, they saw a cat hunched up and miserable sitting on a gate.

"It's a fine day, Cat," they said, "far too fine for you to look so sad."

"It's a bad sad day for me," said the cat. "My owners say I no longer catch as many rats and mice as I did when I was young, so they are replacing me with a kitten. They cannot feed us both, so I am going to be put in a sack and drowned in the river."

"Don't wait for that to happen," said the donkey and the dog. "We are also too old for our masters, but we have not waited to be finished off. We are on our way to Bremen to earn our living as musicians. You still have your voice. Come with us."

The cat uttered a fine "Miaow!" in agreement.

So the three animals journeyed on to Bremen together. At the next farm they met a cock strutting up and down. All his feathers were ruffled out in indignation.

"What's the trouble, Cock?" they asked. "You look upset."

"How would you feel," replied the cock, "if you overheard your mistress planning to wring your neck so she could cook you for dinner on Sunday when they have visitors coming?"

"Come with us to Bremen," said the donkey, the dog and the cat. "We are going to earn our living there as musicians. We're sure you have a fine singing voice."

"Indeed I do," said the cock, and to show them he uttered a loud "Cock-a-doodle-doo!"

It was too far for them to reach Bremen that day, so when evening came they found a sheltered place in a wood to rest for the night. The dog and the donkey settled themselves comfortably at the bottom of a tree, the cat climbed into the branches, and the cock roosted high up at the top. They were all tired, but none of them slept for they were all so hungry.

When it was quite dark the animals saw a light shining from a house they had not noticed before. It made them think of food, and the cat said, "Friends, let's go and investigate. Where there is a house, there may be something to eat."

Together they crept up to one of the windows where a light was shining. The donkey being the tallest looked through first.

"Well, friend, what do you see?" asked the cock.

"I see a table laden with food and drink, and a group of mean-looking men counting piles of money," said the donkey.

The cat, the dog and the cockerel jumped up onto the donkey's back and peered through the window too. They did not realize it but they had discovered a robbers' hideout.

"Let us try out our music," said one of the animals. "If we sing a fine song for them they may give us some of their supper."

Together they all sang. The donkey brayed, the dog barked, the cat yowled and the cock crowed. The noise was tremendous.

The effect was not at all what they expected, for the robbers, hearing this noise, thought they were about to be arrested. They ran helter-skelter as fast as they could into the woods, leaving the doors wide open.

"That was nice of them," said the four animals, when the robbers did not reappear. "They have gone away and left us their home to enjoy."

The donkey found some good hay in the barn and the cock some grain, while the cat and the dog ate all they wanted from the robbers' table. Then they all slept soundly. In time the candles burnt down and went out and the house lay in darkness.

Some hours later, the robbers returned. They had been arguing among themselves, for some thought they had given in too easily, by running away without a fight, while the others thought it was foolish to go back to the house, for they would surely be caught and put in prison. Now they drew nearer, and seeing no sign of life they decided it would be safe for one of them to return and take some of the gold they had left behind.

Quietly the robber crept up to the house, and tried to light a candle. As he did so the cat awoke, and the robber saw his green eyes glowing in the dark. Mistaking them for the embers of the fire, he held a splinter of wood to them.

The cat, thinking he was being attacked, flew at the robber, spitting and scratching for all he was worth. The robber, fearing some great wild beast was attacking him, dropped the wood and ran for his life. In the doorway he tripped over the dog who howled and bit the robber's ankle. The robber limped across the yard where the donkey lashed out at him with his heels. Then the cock, hearing all the commotion and fearing his friends were being killed, flew at the robber with his claws.

The robber fled back to his companions. "It is surely a monster and a devil rolled into one that has taken over our house," he said. "First I was scratched, then bitten, then kicked, and finally attacked from above by fierce talons and whirling feathers. The noise of screeching and howling was enough to wake the dead. We must never go back there again."

So it was that the robbers set off for another part of the country and left their hideout in the woods to the animals. In the morning the four musicians discussed the odd disturbances in the middle of the night. Since the stranger had disappeared they decided to stay where they were for a time.

"We will go to Bremen another day," they said.

But they never did go to Bremen. Instead they lived happily in the house for many years and never tried singing together again.

OLD KING COLE

Old King Cole was a merry old soul,
And a merry old soul was he;
He called for his pipe and he called for his bowl,
And he called for his fiddlers three.

Every fiddler had a fiddle,
And a very fine fiddle had he;
Oh, there's none so rare as can compare
With King Cole and his fiddlers three.

THE QUEEN OF HEARTS

The Queen of Hearts
She made some tarts,
All on a summer's day;
The Knave of Hearts
He stole the tarts,
And took them clean away.

The King of Hearts
Called for the tarts,
And beat the knave full sore;
The Knave of Hearts
Brought back the tarts,
And vowed he'd steal no more.

PUSSY CAT, PUSSY CAT

Pussy cat, pussy cat,
　　Where have you been?
I've been to London
　　To look at the Queen.

Pussy cat, pussy cat,
　　What did you there?
I frightened a little mouse
　　Under her chair.

CHRISTMAS IS COMING

Christmas is coming,
The geese are getting fat,
Please to put a penny
In the old man's hat.
If you haven't got a penny,
A ha'penny will do;
If you haven't got a ha'penny,
Then God bless you!

GUNPOWDER PLOT

Please to remember
The fifth of November,
Gunpowder treason and plot;
I see no reason
Why gunpowder treason
Should ever be forgot.

Puss-in-Boots

A miller once died, leaving his three sons all that he possessed — his mill, his donkey and his cat. They quickly arranged between them that the eldest son should keep the mill, the middle son the donkey, while the youngest should take the cat.

"It is very hard on me," grumbled the youngest son. "My brothers can earn their living with the mill and the donkey, but once I have eaten the cat, I will have nothing."

"Don't talk like that, master," said the cat. "Give me some boots and a sack with a string to tie at the top and you shall see that it was a lucky day for you when you became my master."

The cat quickly went to catch some mice and rats to prove how useful he was, and the miller's son found him the boots and a sack which tied at the top. The cat pulled on the boots and strutted around proudly. Then, taking the sack, he filled it with bran and tempting green leaves and set out for a nearby field where he knew there were rabbits. There he lay down with the sack open beside him and pretended to sleep.

Before long some curious rabbits came to investigate the sleeping cat and the sack, and when they smelt the delicious food they hopped into the sack. In a flash Puss-in-Boots jumped up, pulled the string tight, and caught the rabbits.

Now he strode off to the king's palace and demanded to see the king. "I have a gift for him from my master, the Marquis of Carabas," he announced. This was a name he had made up for the miller's son to impress the king.

"Thank your master for me," said the king, "and tell him I am pleased with his gift."

Some time later Puss-in-Boots set out again with his sack. This time he put a handful of corn in the sack and caught some partridge, and once more he took them to the king's palace, and presented them to the king from the Marquis of Carabas.

Not long afterwards Puss-in-Boots heard that the king was going to drive with his daughter by the river, and he told the miller's son to follow him and do whatever he said. By now the lad realized that Puss was no ordinary cat, and he promised to do everything he was told.

Puss then asked the miller's son to take off his clothes and swim in the river. When the king's carriage came past he called out, "Help! My master, the Marquis of Carabas, is drowning!"

The king, hearing the name of the Marquis, stopped his carriage, and ordered his guards to save the young man. While they were dragging him out, the cat told the king that robbers had run off with his master's clothes. The truth was that Puss had hidden the clothes under a stone. Quickly the king sent one of his servants to fetch some fine clothes, for he remembered the gifts of game Puss had brought to the palace.

When the miller's son put on the new clothes he looked very handsome indeed. The king's daughter immediately fell in love with him, and the king invited him to drive with them.

Puss ran on ahead and found some men working in a field. "The king is about to drive past," he told them. "If he asks you who owns this field, you must answer 'The Marquis of Carabas'. If you don't," he added, "you shall be chopped into little pieces."

A few moments later the king's carriage came along and the king asked the men who owned the land. They remembered the fierce threats from Puss-in-Boots and answered:

"The Marquis of Carabas, Sire."

The king was impressed. Again the cat ran ahead and found some harvesters cutting corn. He told them to say all the fields they were working in belonged to the Marquis of Carabas. If they did not, he said he would make sure they were killed. When the king heard that the Marquis of Carabas owned this land too he was even more impressed.

Meanwhile Puss hurried on to a big castle where a wicked magician lived. The magician was the real owner of the land through which the king and his companions were driving.

The cat knocked at the door and asked to see the magician, and when he met him he bowed very low. "Is it true that you can change yourself into any animal – a lion, a tiger, even an elephant?" he asked with great respect.

"It is true," replied the magician and turned into a great lion. Puss-in-Boots was terrified and only just managed to scramble to safety on a roof – not easy for a cat wearing big boots. There he huddled until the lion changed back into the magician.

"That was truly remarkable," he said to the magician most politely. "But I don't suppose you can also turn yourself into a tiny animal like a mouse or a rat?"

"That's even easier," said the magician, and in a flash he became a tiny mouse, scampering on the floor. With a leap Puss pounced on him and that was the end of the magician.

Just then Puss-in-Boots heard the king's carriage arriving at the castle. He ran outside and said to the king, "Welcome to the house of my master, the Marquis of Carabas."

The king entered with his daughter and the miller's son and looked round the fine castle. Realizing that his daughter already loved the young man, he said, "Tell me, Marquis, what would you say to marrying my daughter?"

The miller's son, who had fallen deeply in love with the princess, bowed very low and accepted. That very same day he married the princess, and you may be sure Puss-in-Boots was always well fed and well looked after for the rest of his life.

DING, DONG, BELL

Ding, dong, bell,
Pussy's in the well.
Who put her in?
Little Johnny Green.
Who pulled her out?
Little Tommy Stout.
What a naughty boy was that
To try to drown poor pussycat,
Who never did him any harm,
But killed the mice in his father's barn.

THE CAT AND THE FIDDLE

Hey diddle, diddle,
The cat and the fiddle,
The cow jumped over the moon;
The little dog laughed
To see such sport,
And the dish ran away with the spoon.

THE WIND

When the wind is in the east,
'Tis good for neither man nor beast;
When the wind is in the north,
The skillful fisher goes not forth;
When the wind is in the south,
It blows the bait in the fishes' mouth;
When the wind is in the west,
Then 'tis at the very best.

Henny Penny

One day Henny Penny was scratching in the farmyard looking for something good to eat when, suddenly, something hit her on the head. "My goodness me!" she said. "The sky must be falling down. I must go and tell the king."

She had not gone far when she met her friend Cocky Locky, and he called out, "Where are you going in such a hurry?"

"I am going to tell the king that the sky is falling down," said Henny Penny.

"I will come with you," said Cocky Locky.

So Henny Penny and Cocky Locky hurried along together towards the king's palace. On the way they saw Ducky Lucky swimming on the pond. "Where are you going?" he called out.

"We are going to tell the king the sky is falling down," replied Henny Penny. "We must go quickly, as there is no time to lose."

"I will come with you," said Ducky Lucky.

So Henny Penny, Cocky Locky and Ducky Lucky hurried on together towards the king's palace. On the way they met Goosey Loosey, who called out, "Where are you all going in such a hurry?"

"We are on our way to tell the king the sky is falling down," said Henny Penny.

"I will come with you," said Goosey Loosey.

So Henny Penny, Cocky Locky, Ducky Lucky and Goosey Loosey hurried on together towards the king's palace.

Round the next corner they met Turkey Lurkey. "Where are you all going on this fine day?" she called out to them.

"It won't be a fine day for long," replied Henny Penny. "The sky is falling down, and we are hurrying to tell the king."

"I will come with you," said Turkey Lurkey.

So Henny Penny, Cocky Locky, Ducky Lucky, Goosey Loosey and Turkey Lurkey went on together towards the king's palace.

Now on their way they met Foxy Loxy who asked, "Where are you going in such a hurry?"

"We are going to the king's palace to tell him the sky is falling down," replied Henny Penny.

"That is a very important message," said Foxy Loxy. "I will come with you. In fact if you follow me I can show you a short cut to the king's palace, so we will get there sooner."

So Henny Penny, Cocky Locky, Ducky Lucky, Goosey Loosey

and Turkey Lurkey all followed Foxy Loxy. He led them to the wood, and up to a dark hole, which was the door to his home. Inside his wife and five hungry children were waiting for him to bring home some dinner.

That, I am sorry to say, was the end of Cocky Locky, Ducky Lucky, Goosey Loosey and Turkey Lurkey, for one by one they all followed Foxy Loxy into his home, and they were all eaten up by the hungry fox family.

Henny Penny was the last to enter the Fox's hole and she heard Cocky Locky crowing in alarm in front of her. Squawking with fright and scattering feathers, she turned and ran as fast as she could for the safety of her own farmyard. There she stayed and she never did tell the king that the sky was falling down.

COCK ROBIN

Who killed Cock Robin?
I, said the sparrow,
With my bow and arrow,
I killed Cock Robin.

Who saw him die?
I, said the fly,
With my little eye,
I saw him die.

Who caught his blood?
I, said the fish,
With my little dish,
I caught his blood.

Who'll make his shroud?
I, said the beetle,
With my thread and needle,
I'll make the shroud.

Who'll dig his grave?
I, said the owl,
With my pick and shovel,
I'll dig his grave.

Who'll be the parson?
I, said the rook,
With my little book,
I'll be the parson.

Who'll be the clerk?
I, said the lark,
If it's not in the dark,
I'll be the clerk.

Who'll carry the link?
I, said the linnet,
I'll fetch it in a minute,
I'll carry the link.

Who'll be chief mourner?
I, said the dove,
I mourn for my love,
I'll be chief mourner.

Who'll carry the coffin?
I, said the kite,
If it's not through the night
I'll carry the coffin.

Who'll bear the pall?
We, said the wren,
Both the cock and the hen,
We'll bear the pall.

Who'll sing a psalm?
I, said the thrush,
As she sat on a bush,
I'll sing a psalm.

Who'll toll the bell?
I, said the bull,
Because I can pull,
I'll toll the bell.

All the birds of the air
Fell a-sighing and a-sobbing,
When they heard the bell toll
For poor Cock Robin.

TO BABYLON

How many miles to Babylon?
Three-score miles and ten.
Can I get there by candle-light?
Yes, and back again.
If your heels are nimble and light,
You may get there by candle-light.

DOCTOR FELL

I do not like thee, Doctor Fell,
The reason why I cannot tell;
But this I know, and know full well,
I do not like thee, Doctor Fell.

The Great Flood

Long, long ago in a far off land there was a great flood. For days and weeks and months it rained and rained and rained. Puddles turned into lakes and tiny streams into great rivers and in time the whole earth was covered with water. This is the story of how it happened.

At that time wicked people lived on the earth. They lived violent, evil lives. God saw this and was deeply hurt.

"I am sorry that I ever made the human race," God said. "I will end the whole dreadful business. I will destroy the people, the animals, the reptiles, the wild birds – everything."

But there was one family who made God pause for a moment. "Noah and his family," thought God. "No! I cannot destroy them. They are good people and love me. I know what I shall do."

Now Noah was a very old man and he and his wife had three sons called Shem, Ham and Japheth, all of whom were married. One day Noah was working in the fields when God appeared to him.

"Build a ship on dry land," God commanded him. "Build it high and broad and long. Make windows in it and a strong door in the side and build it with three decks, each divided into many compartments. Seal it, too, inside and out with pitch and keep it watertight.

"When the time comes, take into this great ark pairs of every animal – reptiles and birds as well – and enough food to feed them all. For I am going to send a flood of water over the whole land. I will destroy everything that lives except you and your family and the creatures with you in the ark."

Noah and his sons began to build the ark as God commanded them. For months they sawed down trees, cut them into planks and hammered them into place. The people who lived around them stared in amazement as the huge ship began to take shape, and laughed at them for working so hard. "Where are you going to sail that?" they jeered. "It's wider than the river."

But Noah and his sons worked on and at last the ship was ready. It had windows all around and a huge door on one side. Inside were three decks, each divided into different rooms. Some of these were filled with food of all kinds — flour and dried fruit, vegetables, grain and stacks of hay. Whatever Noah and his family could find, they stored in the ark.

Now the time came when God told Noah to call the animals and to tell his family to enter the great ship. And now two by two the animals came. There were great cats and tiny mice and the smallest of insects. There were antelope and horses, camels and rhinoceroses, lizards, snakes and tortoises.

It took seven days for them all to arrive and soon the ark was very full indeed. On the seventh day as heavy spots of rain splashed down God told Noah to enter and close the ark.

The clouds grew darker and the rain began to fall more and more heavily. Never before had such rain been seen. It poured like a waterfall from the sky and the seas began to rise. Huge tidal waves flowed over the land, drowning everything in their path. Day after day it rained until all that could be seen was the ark floating on a vast grey sea.

At last the rain fell more gently and slowly the flood began to go down. The animals and Noah's family lived together for five months without sight of anything but water. Now they felt their ship settle on solid ground. They had come to rest on the top of a mountain called Ararat.

Noah peered anxiously out of a window. He and his family and all the animals longed to be on land once more but only the mountain tops could be seen. Everywhere else was still covered with water and Noah did not dare to open the door.

After waiting a while he let a raven out to see if it could find somewhere to settle. It never came back and after a week Noah sent out a dove. The dove flew around but could find nowhere to rest or find food so it came back to the ark. When Noah saw it fluttering outside, he knew the earth must still be covered with water and he let the bird inside.

Another week he waited with all the animals. Then Noah sent out the dove again and this time it returned in the evening with an olive branch in its beak. Now Noah knew the waters were really going down. He waited one more week and again sent out the dove. When it did not return Noah knew it was time to leave the ark. He opened the door a crack and in every direction he saw green grass and trees and flowers.

Noah called his family together and all the animals grew quiet to listen to him.

"The time has come," he told them. "Now we can leave the ark." Then he and his sons pushed open the great door.

Out poured the animals, squawking and barking, neighing and roaring. Out scampered the mice; out ran the rabbits and hares; out leapt the zebras, the sheep and the horses; out stalked the bears too and the stately lions while the birds sang and fluttered overhead. All the animals were glad to be out in the open once more with room to leap or fly or dance or just to curl up in the warm sunshine.

God saw the destruction he had caused and said to Noah:

"I will never again send such a flood. Never again will I destroy all living creatures or curse the land. And as a sign that I shall keep this promise, I give you the rainbow."

Just then a brilliant rainbow arched over the ark and over Noah and his family and all the animals. Ever since that day, whenever the sun comes out in the rain, you will see a rainbow in the sky. It reminds us of God's promise that there will never again be a great flood over the whole earth.

SLEEP, BABY, SLEEP

Sleep, baby, sleep,
  Our cottage vale is deep;
The little lamb is on the green
With woolly fleece so soft and clean,
  Sleep, baby, sleep.

Sleep, baby sleep,
  Down where the woodbines creep;
Be always like the lamb so mild,
A kind and sweet and gentle child,
  Sleep, baby, sleep.

HUSH-A-BYE

Hush-a-bye, baby, on the tree top,
When the wind blows, the cradle will rock;
When the bough breaks, the cradle will fall;
Down will come baby, cradle and all.

NIDDLEDY,
NODDLEDY

Niddledy, noddledy
To and fro,
Tired and sleepy,
To bed we go,

Jump into bed,
Switch off the light,
Head on the pillow,
Shut your eyes tight.

Jack and the Beanstalk

There was once a boy called Jack. His mother thought he was lazy, and she was right. Jack did not like work, but he was brave and quick-witted, as you will see from this story. He lived with his mother in a small cottage and their most valuable possession was their cow, Milky-White. But the day came when Milky-White gave them no milk and Jack's mother said she must be sold.

"Take her to market," she told Jack, "and mind you get a good price for her."

So Jack set out to market leading Milky-White by her halter. After a while he sat down to rest by the side of the road. An old man came by and Jack told him where he was going.

"Don't bother to go to the market," the old man said. "Sell your cow to me. I will pay you well. Look at these beans. Only plant them, and overnight you will find you have the finest bean plants in all the world. You'll be better off with these beans than with an old cow or money. Now, how many is five, Jack?"

"Two in each hand and one in your mouth," replied Jack, as sharp as a needle.

"Right you are, here are five beans," said the old man and he handed the beans to Jack and took Milky-White's halter.

When he reached home, his mother said, "Back so soon, Jack? Did you get a good price for Milky-White?"

Jack told her how he had exchanged the cow for five beans and before he could finish his account, his mother started to shout and box his ears. "You lazy good-for-nothing boy," she screamed, "how could you hand over our cow for five old beans? What will we live on now? We shall starve to death, you stupid boy."

She flung the beans through the open window and sent Jack to bed without his supper.

When Jack woke the next morning there was a strange green light in his room. All he could see from the window was green leaves. A huge beanstalk had shot up overnight. It grew higher than he could see. Quickly Jack got dressed and stepped out of the window right onto the beanstalk and started to climb.

"The old man said the beans would grow overnight," he thought. "They must indeed be very special beans."

Higher and higher Jack climbed until at last he reached the top and found himself on a strange road. Jack followed it until he came to a great castle where he could smell the most delicious breakfast. Jack was hungry. It had been a long climb and he had had nothing to eat since midday the day before. Just as he reached the door of the castle he nearly tripped over the feet of an enormous woman.

"Here, boy," she called. "What are you doing? Don't you know my husband likes to eat boys for breakfast? It's lucky I have already fried up some bacon and mushrooms for him today, or I'd pop you in the frying pan. He can eat you tomorrow, though."

"Oh, please don't let him eat me," pleaded Jack. "I only came to ask you for a bite to eat. It smells so delicious."

Now the giant's wife had a kind heart and did not really enjoy cooking boys for breakfast, so she gave Jack a bacon sandwich. He was still eating it when the ground began to shake with heavy footsteps, and a loud voice boomed: "Fee, Fi, Fo, Fum."

"Quick, hide!" cried the giant's wife and she pushed Jack into the oven. "After breakfast, he'll fall asleep," she whispered. "That is when you must creep away." She left the oven door open a crack so that Jack could see into the room. Again the terrible rumbling voice came:

"Fee, Fi, Fo, Fum,
I smell the blood of an Englishman,
Be he alive or be he dead,
I'll grind his bones to make my bread."

A huge giant came into the room. "Boys, boys, I smell boys," he shouted. "Wife, have I got a boy for breakfast today?"

"No, dear," she said soothingly. "You have got bacon and mushrooms. You must still be smelling the boy you ate last week."

The giant sniffed the air suspiciously but at last sat down. He wolfed his breakfast of bacon and mushrooms, drank a great bucketful of steaming tea and crunched up a massive slice of toast. Then he fetched a couple of bags of gold from a cupboard and started counting gold coins. Before long he dropped off to sleep.

Quietly Jack crept out of the oven. Carefully he picked up two gold coins and ran as fast as he could to the top of the beanstalk. He threw the gold down to his mother's garden and climbed after it. At the bottom he found his mother looking in amazement at the gold coins and the beanstalk. Jack told her of his adventures in the giant's castle and when she examined the gold she realized he must be speaking the truth.

Jack and his mother used the gold to buy food. But the day came when the money ran out, and Jack decided to climb the beanstalk again.

It was all the same as before, the long climb, the road to the castle, the smell of breakfast and the giant's wife. But she was not so friendly this time.

"Aren't you the boy who was here before," she asked, "on the day that some gold was stolen from under my husband's nose?"

But Jack convinced her she was wrong and in time her heart softened again and she gave him some breakfast. Once more as Jack was eating the ground shuddered and the great voice boomed: "Fee, Fi, Fo, Fum." Quickly, Jack jumped into the oven.

As he entered, the giant bellowed:

"Fee, Fi, Fo, Fum,
I smell the blood of an Englishman,
Be he alive or be he dead,
I'll grind his bones to make my bread."

The giant's wife put a plate of sizzling sausages before him, telling him he must be mistaken. After breakfast the giant fetched a hen from a back room. Every time he said "Lay!" the hen laid an egg of solid gold.

"I must steal that hen, if I can," thought Jack, and he waited until the giant fell asleep. Then he slipped out of the oven, snatched up the hen and ran for the top of the beanstalk. Keeping the hen under one arm, he scrambled down as fast as he could.

Jack's mother was waiting but she was not pleased when she saw the hen.

"Another of your silly ideas, is it, bringing an old hen when you might have brought us some gold?"

Then Jack set the hen down carefully, and commanded "Lay!" just as the giant had done. To his mother's surprise the hen laid an egg of solid gold.

Jack and his mother now lived in great luxury. But in time Jack became a little bored and he made up his mind to climb the beanstalk once more.

This time he did not risk talking to the giant's wife in case she recognized him. He slipped into the kitchen when she was not looking, and hid himself in the log basket. He watched the giant's wife prepare breakfast and then he heard the giant's roar:

"Fee, Fi, Fo, Fum,
I smell the blood of an Englishman,
Be he alive or be he dead,
I'll grind his bones to make my bread."

"If it's that cheeky boy who stole your gold and our magic hen, then I'll help you catch him," said the giant's wife. "Why don't we look in the oven? It's my guess he'll be hiding there."

You may be sure that Jack was glad he was not in the oven. The giant and his wife hunted high and low but never thought to look in the log basket. At last they gave up and the giant sat down to breakfast.

After he had eaten, the giant fetched a harp. When he commanded "Play!" the harp played the most beautiful music. Soon the giant fell asleep, and Jack crept out of the log basket. Quickly he snatched up the harp and ran. But the harp called out loudly, "Master, save me! save me!" and the giant woke. With a roar of rage he chased after Jack.

Jack raced down the road towards the beanstalk with the giant's footsteps thundering behind him. When he reached the top of the beanstalk he threw down the harp and started to slither down after it. The giant followed, and now the whole beanstalk shook and shuddered with his weight, and Jack feared for his life. At last he reached the ground, and seizing an axe he chopped at the beanstalk with all his might. *Snap!*

"Look out, mother!" he called as the giant came tumbling down, head first. He lay dead at their feet with the beanstalk on the ground beside them. The harp was broken, but the hen continued to lay golden eggs for Jack and his mother and they lived happily for a long, long time.

PINS

See a pin and pick it up,
All the day you'll have good luck.
See a pin and let it lay,
Bad luck you'll have all the day.

IF WISHES
WERE
HORSES

If wishes were horses,
  Beggars would ride.
If turnips were watches,
  I would wear one by my side.
And if "ifs" and "ands" were pots and pans,
There'd be no work for tinkers!

THE OLD WOMAN IN A SHOE

There was an old woman who lived in a shoe;
She had so many children she didn't know what to do.
She gave them some broth without any bread;
Then whipped them all soundly and put them to bed.

THE MAN WITH NOUGHT

There was a man and he had nought,
  And robbers came to rob him;
He crept up to the chimney pot,
  And then they thought they had him.

But he got down on the other side,
  And then they could not find him;
He ran fourteen miles in fifteen days,
  And never looked behind him.

THE DONKEY

If I had a donkey that wouldn't go,
Would I beat him? Oh, no, no.
I'd put him in the barn and give him some corn.
The best little donkey that ever was born.

The Dragon
and the Monkey

Far away in the China Seas lived a dragon and his wife. She was fretful and rather difficult, but he was a kind and loving dragon. As they swam in the warm seas together she was forever complaining and asking her husband to fetch her different foods. He always thought, "This time I will really make her happy, and then how easy and lovely life will be." Yet somehow, whatever delicacy he fetched her, she was never satisfied and always wanted something else.

One day she twitched her tail more than usual, and told her husband that she was not feeling well and that she had heard a monkey's heart was the only thing to cure her.

"You are certainly looking pale, my love," said the dragon, "and you know I would do anything for you, but how can I possibly find you a monkey's heart? Monkeys live up trees, and I could never catch one."

"Now I know you don't love me." cried his wife. "If you did you would find a way to catch one. Now I shall surely die!"

The dragon sighed and swam off across the seas to an island where he knew some monkeys lived. "Somehow," he thought desperately, "I must trick a monkey into coming with me."

301

When he reached the island, he saw a little monkey sitting in a tree. The dragon called out:

"Hello monkey! It's good to see you! Come down and talk to me. That tree looks so unsafe, you might fall out!"

At that the monkey roared with laughter. "Ha! Ha! Ha! You are funny, dragon. Whoever heard of a monkey falling out of a tree?"

The dragon thought of his wife and tried again.

"I'll show you a tree covered with delicious juicy fruit, monkey. It grows on the other side of the sea."

Again the monkey laughed. "Ha! Ha! Ha! Whoever heard of a monkey swimming across the sea, dragon?"

"I could take you on my back, little monkey," said the dragon.

The monkey liked this idea and swung out of the tree onto the dragon's back. As he swam across the sea, the dragon thought there was no way the monkey could escape, so he said:

"I am sorry, little monkey, I've tricked you. There are no trees with delicious fruit where we are going. I am taking you to my wife who wishes to eat your heart. She says it is the only thing that will cure her of her illness."

The monkey looked at the water all around him and saw no way to escape, but he thought quickly, and said:

"Your poor wife! I am sorry to hear she's not well. There is nothing I'd like more than to give her my heart. But what a pity you did not tell me before we left. You obviously do not know, dragon, that we monkeys never carry our hearts with us. I left it behind in the tree where you found me. If you would be kind enough to swim back there with me, I shall willingly fetch it."

So the dragon turned round and swam back to the place where he had found the monkey. With one leap the monkey was in the branches of the tree, safe out of the dragon's reach.

"I'm sorry to disappoint you, dragon," he called out, "but I had my heart with me all the time. You won't trick me out of this tree again. Ha! Ha! Ha!"

There was no way the dragon could reach him and whether or not he ever caught another monkey I do not know. Perhaps he is still looking while his wife swims alone in the China Seas.

302

MY MOTHER SAID

My mother said, I never should
Play with the gypsies in the wood.
If I did, then she would say:
Naughty girl to disobey.
Your hair shan't curl and your shoes
  shan't shine,
You gypsy girl you shan't be mine.
And my father said that if I did,
He'd rap my head with the teapot lid.

COCK A DOODLE DOO

Cock a doodle doo!
My dame has lost her shoe,
My master's lost his fiddle stick
And knows not what to do.

Cock a doodle doo!
What is my dame to do?
Till master finds his fiddle stick
She'll dance without her shoe.

OLD MOTHER SHUTTLE

Old Mother Shuttle,
    Lived in a coal scuttle
Along with her dog and her cat;
    What they ate I can't tell,
    But 'tis known very well
That not one of the party was fat.

Old Mother Shuttle
    Scoured out her coal scuttle,
And washed both her dog and her cat;
    The cat scratched her nose,
    So they came to hard blows,
And who was the gainer by that?

Anansi and Common Sense

You may already know that Anansi is a spider, an impudent spider, full of tricks and surprises, but did you know that Anansi is responsible for the fact that everyone – or almost everyone – has a little bit of common sense? This is how it happened.

Anansi was feeling full of importance one day, and thought the cleverest thing he could do was to collect up all the common sense in the world and keep it safe in one place. So he scuttled here and scuttled there, gathering it up in a great calabash. He then plugged the calabash with a roll of dried leaves.

"There," he said to himself, "is all the common sense in the world. Whenever I need it I shall be able to help myself, and my enemies will have none. I *shall* have fun for I shall always get the better of them." He really was pleased with himself.

"Hey, wait a minute though," he thought, "where can I keep it safe? Everyone will want to steal it from me. I know, I'll put the calabash at the top of that great coconut tree. None of the other animals will ever find it."

So Anansi got a long rope and tied it around the calabash, and then he looped the other end of the rope around his head. The calabash hung down in front of him, leaving all his legs free to climb the tree.

Well, Anansi started to climb the tree, but it was not easy as the calabash kept bumping around between him and the trunk of the tree. Slowly he inched up on his eight legs until, suddenly, when he was about half way up, he heard laughter.

Now there is nothing Anansi hates more than being laughed at. Looking down he saw a small boy and the small boy was laughing his head off.

"Fancy climbing a tree with the calabash in front of you, Anansi!" he called out. "Surely you know that if you want to climb a tree with a calabash, it is more sensible to put the calabash on your back."

Anansi quivered with annoyance. In fact he was furious, for what the small boy said was common sense, yet hadn't he, Anansi, collected all the common sense in the world and stuffed it into the calabash?

In a rage he flung the calabash to the foot of the tree, where it shattered. The common sense inside was scattered into little pieces and blown all over the world, and everyone, or nearly everyone, got a little bit. So when you show you have some common sense, remember you have Anansi the Spider to thank for it.

MOSES

Moses supposes his toeses are roses,
But Moses supposes erroneously;
For nobody's toeses are posies of roses
As Moses supposes his toeses to be.

HUSH, MY BABY

Hush, my baby, do not cry,
Papa's coming by and by;
When he comes he'll come in a gig,
Hi cockalorum, jig, jig, jig.

HUSH THEE

Hush thee, my baby,
Lie still with thy daddy,
Thy mammy has gone to the mill,
To get some meal
To bake a cake,
So pray, my dear baby, lie still.

WILLIE WINKIE

Wee Willie Winkie runs through the town,
Upstairs and downstairs in his nightgown,
Rapping at the window, crying through the lock,
Are all the children in their beds? It's past ten o'clock.

The Princess and the Pea

There was once a handsome prince who wanted to marry a princess. He travelled far and wide to find one and met a great many people, and quite a number of princesses, too. The trouble was that something was wrong with all the princesses, and after many months he returned home and told his parents, "I cannot find a princess to marry."

One night, not long after his return, a terrible storm broke over the palace. Lightning flashed, thunder crashed and the rain poured down. The prince and his parents heard someone knocking on the great front door. "Who would be out in such a storm?" they asked each other.

A girl stood shivering on the doorstep. Water streamed off her hair and down her face and her dress was soaked through. "Come in," cried the king. "Come in and tell us who you are."

"I am a p-p-p-princess," she replied through her chattering teeth. "I was looking for the king's palace, and I was caught in a storm." She did not look in the least like a princess, but the queen said to herself, "I believe I can find out if she is a princess or not."

While the girl was having a hot bath the queen went to prepare her bedroom. She sent two maids scurrying to collect mattresses and quilts from all over the palace. First she placed a dried pea underneath the bottom mattress and then more and more mattresses were piled onto the bed. In all twenty mattresses were placed on top of the pea. Then the queen told the maids to place twenty feather quilts on top of the mattresses. When the girl went to the bedroom she found her bed so high that she had to climb a ladder to get into it.

The next morning both the king and queen asked if she had slept well. "I am sorry to say, I had a very bad night," she told them. "There was a little hard lump in my bed and I tossed and turned all night. Now I am black and blue with bruises."

The queen was delighted. Only a real princess could have felt a pea through twenty mattresses and twenty quilts. She hurried off to tell the prince.

The prince married the princess and they lived happily for many years. As for the pea, it was put on display in a glass case in the town museum. When they saw it, people would say, "That really is some story, the story of the princess and the pea."

HUSH, LITTLE BABY

Hush, little baby, don't say a word,
Papa's going to buy you a mocking bird.

If the mocking bird won't sing,
Papa's going to buy you a diamond ring.

If the diamond ring turns to brass,
Papa's going to buy you a looking glass.

If the looking glass gets broke,
Papa's going to buy you a billy goat.

If that billy goat runs away,
Papa's going to buy you another today.

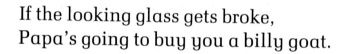

BEDTIME

The Man in the Moon
Looked out of the moon,
Looked out of the moon and said,
'Tis time for all children on the earth
To think about getting to bed!

A PRAYER

Send Daddy home
With a fiddle and a drum,
A pocket full of spices,
An apple and a plum.

Index of First Lines